Marquel's
REDEMPTION

OTHER WORKS BY EMILY W. SKINNER

Novels by Emily W. Skinner

Marquel

Marquel's Dilemma

Marquel's Redemption

Booktrailer:
Marquel book trailer on YouTube—
featuring actor Eric Roberts & Marquel Skinner
www.youtube.com/watch?v=6e6O7iYqeVQ

Young Adult Novels by E. W. Skinner

St. Blair: Children of the Night

St. Blair: Sybille's Reign

St Blair: The Diary of St. Blair

Marquel's
REDEMPTION

By Emily W. Skinner

For Ellen, a beautiful sister whose honesty and friendship I cherish. I love you!

CHAPTER ONE

"Sexually harass me, boss. I won't press charges," Joanne's live-in bodyguard boogied toward her. Dabs of shaving cream framed his chiseled grin.

Rick Jones cranked up Marvin Gaye's *Sexual Healing* and danced for Joanne. Arms raised, he snapped his fingers and gyrated his hips in a circular motion as he approached her desk.

Joanne heard him, but was busy enough at her task to ignore him.

He wasn't her type, which made their living arrangement possible.

Jones' short, sandy hair was cropped in a medium fade, slightly longer on the top with a smooth side part. His uniform: belted cargo pants, black underwear, close fitting black t-shirt, work boots, and a leather bomber jacket—weather permitting.

Young, retired military, Jones was a creature of routine. A beefy fighting champ and hero in the Persian Gulf war. A human Rock' Em Sock' Em Robot.

The man who saved her life.

He was nothing like George or Zach.

Neither of Joanne's former husbands had Jones' egotistical charm.

Confidence was Rick's primary weapon.

Aside from his bounty-hunting/bodyguard career, which he visibly loved, he also loved to sing bad karaoke, line dance and grill meat. His impromptu dance routines were often timed with Joanne's darker moods. It wasn't his job to divert her attention, but she felt he did so because he didn't like to see her sad.

Joanne stopped typing.

"Zach liked Motown," she pulled off her glasses and rolled her chair back.

Jones reached out his hand.

She acquiesced.

Jones pulled her close. "This is for Zach."

He spun Joanne around, dipped her, then quickly brought her back to her feet and returned her to her seat. Snapping his fingers, he swayed into his freestyle again.

Joanne crossed her arms and smiled, she lacked transition in these moments. Jones' hip gyrations carried him toward the hallway to complete his morning routine.

He had charisma, she had to admit.

The music made her think of Zach, but the dip had a negative effect. It was a muscle memory. She felt nervous instead of excited—she had not been held in a very long time.

The term "failure to thrive" came to mind.

She recalled hearing a hospital worker discussing this while she was in a coma.

The realization stunned her. Like a spark in time.

She associated her feeling now with the discussion she heard while unconscious.

The nurses talked about holding a "failure to thrive" infant in an attempt to provide the nurturing the baby needed to grow and develop.

In Rick's embrace Joanne felt a physical connectedness that her body, mind and spirit needed. A reason to live—grow, develop...

She touched her abdomen, remembering the wound that sent her, and ultimately Zach, to the same hospital on the same fateful day. She then thought about carrying little Marquel, the pregnancy that she and George had cherished many years before.

The music became white noise in her ears.

It seemed she could go deep in a moment, moving from pleasure to shame and horror.

A touch on her shoulder brought her back. She took a breath.

"Boss?" Jones said, a few times.

Her startled expression wasn't new, nor were her reactions. He could never figure out what the trigger was.

"Grab a bite?" He found it easier to distract her. He wasn't her therapist.

Joanne nodded.

"Chinese, Mexican, Italian?"

"Is it racist to talk food like that?" Her smile was back.

"Humph," Rick scratched his head. "Well, I guess if we pick one over another, it might be considered discrimination? But in a good way... right?"

"You decide."

"Mexican it is," he exclaimed. "A little Mariachi music, a margarita... some enchiladas." Fingertips to his lips he kissed the air. "Yes!"

"Mexicans save the day," she thought that came out awkward. She blushed.

He gave her a wink and whistled his way back to his room.

She wasn't certain how to feel at moments like this. The wink was innocent, but stirring. She knew he wasn't flirting. Even the dance was just Rick being Rick. And live-in bodyguard wasn't his usual detail, he had only taken the job to help her transition after trauma.

Sometimes it seemed her life was merely trauma followed by transitions...

Joanne put her glasses back on and looked at the three small photos on her desk, each a tombstone in her mind.

George, Zach and little Marquel.

She rearranged them to give Marquel her own space.

She'd sort the men out later.

The photos represented the work she had to complete. Healing those chapters would help her live awhile longer—at least until they were all together again.

CHAPTER TWO

Humberto Vasquez had a visitor. He heard the electric door closing behind him as he moved toward a bank of phones, sectioned for each visitor pairing.

A buzzer sounded. The locking mechanism behind him groaned uncharacteristically, causing his attending guard to do a double-take before the door sealed itself. The guard then returned his attention to Humberto, who had taken his seat.

Humberto's long black hair was pulled back in a rubber band. His fixed snarl was a permanent expression since his incarceration.

He was no longer the youthful, carefree Colombian arrested on Mt. Lee.

Humberto was heavier now from the starchy foods the prison served, tanned dark from his time in the yard, and a beast from working out. Physical activity never interested him as a cartel leader, but now exercise kept him focused and revered.

He needed to stay strong to keep the Mexican Mafia in their place and off his back.

Both the Colombian and Mexican cartels had a huge business inside and outside the southern California prison.

The Mexicans being the majority, and Humberto still the new kid on the block.

The Mexicans cut deals as inmates flocked to the cheapest fix.

Loyalty, both cartels discovered, was not a tenet of addiction. And Humberto's rival would not be undersold.

Juan Carlos Gallo had already served 30 years of a life sentence, was twenty years Humberto's senior, and the leader of Mexico's largest crime family, the Gallo Cartel.

Gallo was as menacing as he was colorful. He was small and barrel-gutted, straight-nosed with a crooked smile, a soft Dracula hairline and showing signs of heart disease. He studied French with a Catholic priest who ministered to inmates weekly. Which gave him the idea to expand his operation to Canada—he wanted Quebec, then all of Canada.

He frequently requested French films and books from his visitors, though most were confiscated and destroyed as many had small packets of cocaine embedded inside.

Gallo was the Drug Enforcement Agency's biggest target. He controlled the largest drug trafficking operation in North America.

The DEA's alias for Gallo was *the mime* as they discovered he spoke in sign language to his gang inside to keep their plans out of earshot—and given his enthusiasm for all things French, including *Marcel Marceau.*

The guards and DEA couldn't control the flow of illegal substances that moved through the prison system, as they soon learned from their closed circuit monitors. It was the best inside crime show, televised live for their daily viewing. They watched, learned, and followed the supply chain. It was only a matter of time before they moved in.

Humberto nodded to the guard and grabbed the phone.

He received hundreds love letters each month from desperate women wanting a dangerous and famous someone in their lonely lives.

He accepted only one visitor.

The happy young woman on the other side of the glass partition was dressed especially trashy for the occasion.

He watched her bounce with enthusiasm.

Black eyeliner complemented her dilated pupils. Her navy blue hair was pulled into a high pony tail. Alabaster skin peeked out from the slashes in her faded black jeans and the rips in her layered neon tees.

Humberto shuddered.

Something about her reminded him of the stories his grand-mother told him of *Madremonte*, a female monster who lured children into her cave and left their parents to roam like zombies in search of their babies.

She grabbed the phone, giggling, "Humby!"

He said nothing.

"Do you like my new color?" She twisted her ponytail in her left hand. "Different from my pictures. Very Addams Family..."

Humberto listened, took a deep breath.

"Say something!" She put a finger in her mouth and sucked on it.

She was already getting on his nerves.

"I'm not stayin' if you're just gonna sit there," Marnie Sikes pouted.

"Joanne?" He asked.

"What about her?" Marnie shrugged.

Humberto moved to hang up the phone.

"God, you're pushy. Aren't you happy to see me?"

He stared.

Marnie waved her hand in front of glass as if to say, *you there?* Her fingernails were chewed up, exposing pink flesh. She had blue ballpoint lines and diagrams drawn in the palms of her hands.

He could only think about Marquel, the star who stole his heart and the hearts of his people in telecasts of the American soap Suburban Life... *Vida Suburbana.*

Her two seasons consisted of 42 episodes translated and re-broadcast in sindicación. His father followed the *telenovela,* and the *el tabloide* stories that were even greater drama than the *series de televisión*

Carlos Vasquez had required everyone in his organization to watch the show. He had the American *tabloide* Pursuit cut up and placed in a scrapbook that he studied daily.

Her true story was a *telenovela* come to life.

He told his son Humberto he would rescue this beautiful star and make her his wife, *hermosa estrella para su esposa*.

Soon Humberto wanted her, too. Everyone in the cartel was indoctrinated into believing she could be their Eva María Duarte de Perón—albeit in the Vasquez way. The *Evita* of their cartel. But only in name. As men would control the organization, while Marquel would be their trophy.

And they... her saviors.

What Marquel meant to him, his father, and their people gave Humberto purpose. When his father died, Humberto's existence became centered around *his* future bride.

He had failed to capture her on Mt. Lee, but in time he would bring her to Colombia... and she would love him.

And he would restore her name again to Marquel as they began their lives together—for his people. He would find a way.

Marnie giggled.

"Where is Joanne?" He asked.

"Her stepdaughter, my best friend Jackie—is being a bitch—*again*. I'm working on it. I think Joanne is still at her therapist's house."

Humberto shook his head. "Not there."

Marnie's eyes got big, "If you know so much, why are you asking me?"

"Your friend doesn't trust you."

"Because she's a bitch! Weren't you listening? Hum-ber-to!"

He grit his teeth. "I have people on the streets."

She shot him a bird. "They aren't doing their job if you're relying on me."

He stared, then broke out laughing.

The guard took note. He had not seen this prisoner smile.

Humberto wagged a finger at Marnie, "This Jackie avoids you. Because you have no class."

"Fuck you, Hum-ber-to."

"I am Vasquez!" He slammed a fist on the glass wall.

The guard stepped in. "This visit is over!"

Humberto glowered at the guard, speaking through clenched teeth, "My apologies."

"Wrap it up." The guard held his stance.

Marnie laughed, "You are a fucking criminal, Hum-ber-to."

His nostrils flared as he spoke, "Vasquez are powerful, unlike your Addams Family."

"Duh. You're a fucking drug cartel." She shot him another bird, "I'm not afraid of you."

He nodded. He liked that.

Her smile was coy, "What do you really want, Humby?

"Bring Joanne."

Marnie rolled her eyes. "Right! Because all I have to do is *ask* my best friend's stepmom, the woman you were trying to kidnap, to just come visit you? Right. She'll jump on that..."

"Do this for me," he said in a low whisper.

Marnie's dark eyes glimmered. His accent was so sexy.

"...and I will marry you, Marnie."

Her mouth dropped.

He nodded again.

"You're serious?" She chewed on the tip of her ponytail.

Humberto licked his lips.

Marnie squealed. "Ohmygod. You *are* serious."

"I will take care of you, Marnie. Do this for me."

"Stop..." she bounced in her chair, "You're making me so horny."

"My fearless *princesa*." He put a hand on his heart.

No one had ever given her credit for her courage. Especially after her creepy-crawly bust at Isabel's house. She was rather proud of her breaking and entering skills, though her parents had her records expunged.

Her mind was blown. What if she hadn't begun writing to him after his arrest? She wouldn't be at this spot. Being proposed to!

While his letters to her were short and often cryptic four sentence replies, she wrote epistles and clearly didn't care if his mail was monitored.

He whispered, keeping his hand on his heart, "I'll see you *and* Joanne next time."

Then he hung up his phone and was escorted out by the guard.

Marnie sat stunned. Her mind's wheels turning... *Jackie would shit,* was all she could think for a minute. She had to get Joanne Manning here, that was it. Then she would be queen of the cartel. Mrs. *Humberto* Fucking Vasquez!

Sophie Krentz woke herself snorting. She opened her eyes in the dimly lit room and realized where she was.

It was massage day. She was home.

Thank goodness...

Her regular masseuse Helga was working on her ankles and feet. Helga found a ticklish spot on the arch of her right foot that startled Sophie. She pulled her foot away.

"Sorry," Helga said.

Sophie laughed. "How long have I been I out?"

"Pretty much the whole time." Helga added some oil to her large hands, warming it by rubbing them together before wrapping them around Sophie's shin.

"I shouldn't drink." Sophie rubbed her eyes.

"You need to detox. We'll do a wrap next week," Helga's tone was stern.

Sophie slapped her round stomach. The sound of a hollow barrel resonated in her ears. "I'm too fat," she rolled to her side.

"What you are doing?" Helga's hands went up.

"I'm done. Pack up. Just help me off this table first," Sophie's short round body could barely touch the floor.

Helga grabbed Sophie's robe and helped her down.

"Drink plenty of water tonight."

Sophie pushed the robe away and crawled into her bed, between the violet satin sheets. "I'm exhausted. Could you lock the door when you leave?"

The bedside phone rang. She grabbed the cordless receiver, "Sophie speaking."

Helga stripped the sheets off the folding massage table, tossing them into Sophie's hamper.

Sophie struggled to talk as she grabbed some cash from her bedside table, "Honey, I'm sorry. I'm staying in bed tonight."

Her naked body began to slide back out of the bed and Helga responded by pushing Sophie toward the middle of the mattress.

This brought laughter from Sophie, "Oh my God, I'm beat."

The masseuse left the room as Sophie rambled to her caller, "I'm attending a gallery opening tomorrow. We'll talk in the morning."

She wasn't yet certain who would be her escort for the occasion. She preferred her date be literate when the event was more than a photo op.

Helga returned with a pitcher of ice water and poured Sophie a tumbler, offering her the glass.

Sophie waved it off and pushed a wad of bills into Helga's hand, blowing her a kiss.

Helga stuffed her pockets and grabbed her equipment.

"Water!" She repeated as she was leaving.

Sophie slid down to a flat position, returning her attention to the caller, "Not tonight, Javier." Her boys were actors who accompanied her to charity functions and dinners. The young man on the other end of the phone was new to Hollywood, and quite lonely.

She was wiped out, therefore unsympathetic, "I'm going now. You can't come over."

He continued to beg.

Thanks to Isabel, Sophie's escorts were being seen at more A-List functions, and becoming quite spoiled as a result.

"Honey, I know you too well. You say we're just going to cuddle and watch movies, but you always get your way." She was too tired for sex.

She never understood why most big girls were lonely. There were plenty of young men looking for a non-judgmental lover who would let them experiment, play... and that Sophie did. Especially after red carpet events. They were very eager to make her happy.

"Listen, I've got to go—No!" Sophie clicked off the cordless phone.

It was almost 5 pm. She still needed to order flowers for the gallery opening but couldn't decide if she wanted to send an arrangement or a tree. She preferred a tree, it was becoming her signature. She wanted to believe she was reforesting the smoggy city of L.A. one lanai at a time.

CHAPTER THREE

"Share this with Judith, please," Greta's eyes teared up in response to Joanne's latest fears. Their regular brunches often led them into more serious conversation, she hoped to lighten the mood by asking, "How's Rick?"

Joanne snapped, "Am I just your girlfriend's patient?"

Greta said nothing, but noted the mention of Rick had preceded Joanne's tone. Her home had been Joanne's refuge through the media circus that followed Zach's death and Joanne's recovery from gunshot wounds. Greta's lover Judith the therapist Joanne had come to rely on...

"I don't expect you to be an AA sponsor—but a friend." Joanne took a sip of mint tea.

Greta's mouth dropped, "Did Judith tell you?"

Joanne wasn't listening. Her head was pounding.

Greta stared her down. "AA!?" she demanded.

Joanne shook her head, no. She wasn't clear what Greta was implying, only that her friend was upset about something.

Greta got up and left the café. She had parked out front and wasted no time tearing out.

Joanne's eyes followed the Jaguar until it was out of view, then found their way to Rick Jones. He was watching her from another café across the street.

He was close enough to protect her and far enough away to give her privacy. Always. She wasn't sure if it was his closeness setting her off these days, or the distance that all but ached between them.

She paid her check, and as she moved from her table to the sidewalk outside he began working his detail, following her discreetly. The observant might think him a stalker. The average person wouldn't notice him at all.

She saw a clothing store she knew Jackie would like. Maybe she'd pick up a gift. Then she thought of her own daughter, wondering what she would be like as a young adult.

Would Marquel be fashionable, or prefer modest styles like Joanne?

Joanne figured Marquel would be a trendsetter, knowing children are usually their parent's opposite.

She entered the retailer. A beautiful young Asian girl asked if she could help Joanne.

This felt like therapy, she inhaled.

"Yes, what is the most popular clothing style for girls your age?"

The young woman's eyes got bright. "Oh, right this way."

The clerk led her to a mannequin adorned in an oversized hounds-tooth print vest, a tailored white shirt and a tutu skirt of black and white tulle. "Very Gwen Stefani," the girl said.

Joanne smiled, "I'll take it."

"What size?"

"What size do you wear?" Joanne asked.

"I'm a four but this runs a little small, so a six would be best." The clerk didn't waste time, grabbing the pieces from a nearby rack before Joanne could answer.

Joanne nodded. "Six it is."

As the girl directed Joanne to the register, the shop bell rang. It was Rick.

"Look what I found for Marquel," she held up the vest and skirt as the clerk wrapped the accompanying blouse.

Rick overlooked what he considered a Freudian slip. "You think Jackie will wear it?"

The clerk's mouth dropped, "You're her."

Joanne felt tension in her neck.

"I'm Joanne Manning," she sighed.

"I know, but you *were* the actress Marquel. Are you doing a new show? Do you have to lose weight?" The girl took the garment from Joanne. "No offense, but I think you're the next size up. I don't want you to be disappointed."

Joanne stopped her, presenting her credit card. "It's not for me. Can you keep a secret?"

The girl nodded.

"Forget I was here."

The girl mimicked sealing her lips and went back to wrapping the purchase.

"Greta okay?" Rick asked Joanne. "She left in a hurry."

Joanne shrugged. "She asked about you."

Rick pulled a pack of gum out of the side pocket of his cargo pants and offered Joanne and the clerk a piece. Both women turned him down.

He unwrapped a stick, folding it into his mouth, chewing and snapping. Joanne associated his chewing as an extension of his thinking. She remembered him chewing gum and talking through the showdown with Vasquez, Collins and bounty hunter Mr. X on Mt. Lee.

The clerk returned Joanne's card and handed her a ribbon-handled shopping bag overspilling with tissue paper.

Rick took the bag instead. "Where to next?"

She noted the frilly purchase dangling from his hand did nothing to diminish his masculinity, it may even have amplified it. *Damn it.*

"Home." Joanne walked swiftly ahead of him.

Once they were outside he fell in step beside her.

She shifted focus again, "I think this outfit is so Marquel."

"You mean Jackie."

"No Rick, I don't mean Jackie," she stopped him. "I thought of buying Jackie something, but I wanted to experience shopping for my daughter. I think she'd be fun and quirky."

He nodded.

"This is going in my closet. When I see it, I'll think of the delightful woman my little girl would be." Her smile was hopeful, her eyes watered.

"I get it," Rick was matter-of-fact. "I have no children—that I'm aware of—but I think there is something to be said for shrine items."

Joanne's eyes lit, "I like that. Shrine. Where do you think Marquel would travel?"

Jones was quick to reply, "No clue."

He didn't want to encourage an adventure.

"Let's go to the newsstand," Joanne looped her arm through his.

From a distance a photographer snapped several photos.

The hair on Jones' neck was up. Something felt off. He glanced around.

The photographer stepped into an alcove as Jones looked in his direction.

Rick continued walking with Joanne. He wanted someone on their back. Clark Roberts perhaps, his partner in the security firm had been his eyes on Mt. Lee the night Joanne was kidnapped by Collins and stalked by Humberto Vasquez. He'd call Roberts later today.

Joanne sensed his change. "What is it, Rick?"

Jones didn't believe in keeping his clients out of the process. His colleagues in the profession felt it important to make the client happy, even clueless of possible danger. Rick was honest, perhaps to a fault.

"We're being watched," Rick said.

He felt her arm tense up as they crossed the street. The small newsstand was a few yards in front of them.

"Paparazzi?" She asked.

"Paparazzi would be in front of us, not tailing us."

Joanne went into the store. Rick faced the exterior while Joanne shopped.

The store was long and narrow, with one center aisle and racks of magazines and newspapers lining the walls. She was looking for travel magazines, but couldn't help noticing *The Beverly Hills* magazine with Isabel and Lyle Herlbert on the cover.

Zach's ex-wife was living the life. The cover featured Lyle's entertainment practice and Isabel's part in public relations, the headline *Power Couple* emblazoned over their airbrushed photo.

Joanne and Isabel had once been members of the same social circle, until Joanne and Zach became a couple, at which point Marquel—Joanne's stage name—became public enemy one to Isabel. Though it wasn't long before Isabel coveted the notoriety the "Marquel" scandal represented.

Once Marquel's secret and Joanne's real name were revealed, Isabel's star rose almost as quickly as her desired limelight.

The media pit the women against each other in one headline after another. Isabel tried to keep her daughter Jackie away from the actress and control custody while Zach and his wives, past and present, became gossip magazine fodder. Exactly what he had tried to avoid.

Joanne turned *The Beverly Hills* magazine over so it wouldn't be visible. She grabbed a *Conde Nast Traveler* and a few other magazines then moved toward the register.

It felt good to have a project to work on.

Judith Wright, Joanne's therapist, wanted her to write her memoirs as part of the recovery, but Joanne couldn't embrace the memories of George and Zach just yet.

This felt more organic. She'd work on Marquel.

The trauma of Joanne's fugue state and total recall of her past when her estranged husband George found her—in a relationship with Zach—was only one of the nightmares she endured in recent years. Knowing she caused each man to question their place in her heart, while also remembering the horror of her daughter's accidental death, was a humiliation she wasn't certain she'd survive. Yet she survived them all.

Punishment. Perhaps a curse.

Judith assured Joanne she'd survived for a reason. A purpose.

By bonding with her daughter's spirit, Joanne hoped for redemption. A way to give her daughter a place in her life and heal from the wounds of trying to suppress her own core personality. The Joanne personality.

Joanne gazed at Rick, holding his on-duty stance just inside the entry—as well as her bright yellow shopping bag. His well-muscled back to her, she could appreciate his masculine form without his knowledge. A rarity, because so few events in her life these days escaped his knowledge. She was grateful he was there.

She paid the clerk and took her purchase.

Judith had assured Joanne that she would heal with time.

It seemed she had nothing but time.

CHAPTER FOUR

Jackie and Josh eyed engagement rings in a small jewelry store on the outskirts of Beverly Hills.

They agreed to keep it simple. She didn't want surprises or skywriting.

He wanted to spoil her, but she wouldn't let him.

Still a resident physician, Josh wanted to buy his future bride the best. The best he could afford, anyway.

"I think I like square cut," Jackie pointed to a white diamond set in silver. She admired its wide, unpolished wedding band.

The jeweler pulled the set out of the glass case and placed them before her.

Josh watched her study the options.

"So... how does this work?" Josh asked the jeweler.

"We have a finance plan, if needed. You'll want the rings sized. We can also engrave the inside of the bands if you like. Have you set a date?"

Jackie gave Josh a stern look.

"Not yet," he shrugged.

She didn't want anyone to know their plans, especially her mother.

Isabel would attempt to take over, alert the media. That was the last thing Jackie needed.

They hoped to start a family soon after Josh completed his residency, maybe even joining a private practice in the interim.

Meanwhile Jackie would continue working behind the scenes at design firm FieldHause Interiors, inventorying fabrics and home accessories until the baby came.

Her bosses, interior designers Joseph Field and Hermann Hause, gave Jackie the liberty to set her own hours and pay herself the salary she deemed fair.

Recommended by Evan, Jackie's pseudo-uncle, the designers were grateful for her organizational skills. Neither Field nor Hause had patience for implementing—or following—systems.

They were the creative team, Jackie their warehouse manager.

Since Jackie had expressed a need to keep her job out of the press and away from prying family members (AKA Isabel) the designers kept their end of the bargain initially by disguising Isabel's existing account and their communications with her in a covert Mission Impossible style approach.

Hermann Hause adored Isabel's gossip and gave her the code name Scarlett Kennedy. The men joked that Isabel was every bit the opportunist of *Gone With The Wind*'s Scarlett when she married her second husband, Frank Kennedy. Like Scarlett, Isabel was all about taking over her husband's business, though Lyle had enough Rhett Butler in him to keep her in check.

To their amazement, Jackie didn't recall their designing her childhood bedroom—and most of Zach and Isabel's home while she was growing up. Ever discreet regarding their client base, the pair often lunched with Isabel—or *Scarlett*—and conveniently neglected to tell Jackie.

While they had hoped to keep their relationship with her mother secret, both men doubted the jig would last, and therefore eventually confessed their madness to Jackie—much to her amusement. They assured their young employee that they had no intention of sharing any confidence Jackie might entrust to them.

She and Josh dined with Isabel and Lyle infrequently by design; her stepfather considered dining out in posh restaurants a part of his business. Jackie didn't mind that Josh was spoiled by the expensive restaurants, only that her mother was always quick to invite loitering photographers to snap a few shots "to keep our name on everyone's lips, dear".

At such times Jackie understood why Joanne had distanced herself from everyone after moving out of Greta and Judith's pool house. But as Jackie grieved the loss of her father, she soon realized she needed people. A family, of sorts. She turned to Joanne's ex-agent Ken and his lover Evan after losing her father. Both had been with Jackie the day Zach died...

"Do you like this one?" Jackie marveled at the ring, "I need a manicure."

He got close enough to examine. "I never noticed your freckles. I think this is the big dipper," he traced the pattern over her knuckles.

She was used to his inability to be serious. "Are we gold or silver people?"

"Can we be both?" Josh asked. "I'm not sure what the children will be?"

The jeweler snapped to attention, "I have just the thing."

Jackie splayed her fingers and Josh pointed to the space between them.

"No webbing, she's a purebred."

She rolled her eyes as the jeweler smiled patiently, placing several gold and silver combinations in front of them.

"No." Jackie's response was immediate.

Josh was surprised, "Really?"

"They look like mistakes."

"Which would make us...?" Josh winced.

"Silver people," Jackie was firm.

Josh put his hand over his heart. "That was close."

CHAPTER FIVE

Isabel felt a tingling in her right arm as she reached to shake her client's hand. It was the same symptom she had been ignoring off and on for several weeks.

Her smile was automatic, "Lyle will meet you in the conference room shortly. Can we offer you..." She knew not to offer wine; this client had just returned from rehab.

"Love," the Brit looked weary, "I'm dying for a tea."

Isabel turned to her assistant, Becky, "Robbie would like some hot tea."

The younger woman nodded and moved toward the kitchen. Becky had stocked the office pantry with all their clients' favorites.

Isabel liked to believe it was her own meticulousness that made Becky so efficient, but her assistant was truly a natural. She learned everyone's preferences because that was her job, but the spreadsheets she created—even the interior cupboard doors marked by client and complete with inventory order forms—were her own. Any perishables that didn't get consumed within a few weeks of the expiration date Becky sent to shelters in the area.

Thus The Herlbert Firm were always ready for a client's surprise visit, such as this one.

Isabel led the rock star to one of the smaller meeting rooms. "How are you?"

"Bloody tired. I want to see my kids."

Isabel was familiar with the faux custody battle.

Robbie Rocket was embroiled in a publicity stunt concocted by his new bride Melody Mars. Mars and Rocket got together when the rocker performed at a political rally for Mars' then husband, Kansas congressman Jim Hanson.

"How old are the twins?" Isabel made polite conversation. Just a formality, of course, because she always knew the answers before she asked the questions.

"Oh Jesus, two? Three? Their still little fuckers," Rocket laughed.

The Rockets had only been married six months but had lived together during the Hanson divorce proceedings and birth of their twin son and daughter.

Isabel waited for Becky to join them. She didn't like for clients to be unattended.

"Urie and Mercury miss you, I'm sure," Isabel's tone was designed to console. Even if it appeared she knew more about the pair than their father did.

Rocket had collapsed on tour in Japan sixty days earlier while Melody was exploiting herself and the children at a Northern Lights photo shoot in Iceland.

Rocket fidgeted in his seat. "The kids are with her mum. Mel nearly froze her nipples off."

Isabel had seen the photos. Lyle was handling the Rockets' legal, the "nipple" shots having been sold by a photographer's rogue assistant.

Eager to launch her new lingerie line in a country that aligned with her planetary family names, Melody decided her eco-friendly cotton bra and panties would be best displayed in the light of the Icelandic auroras boreales. But exposure sent her areolas to a hospital in Reykjavik at the same time Robbie was in a Tokyo infirmary.

Their dual hospitalizations had greater impact than her divorce stunt. A master manipulator, the model was sure her lingerie company would gain sympathy and free press if she were a struggling single mother of twins.

Rocket reluctantly agreed to the scheme, though he was not sure if she was setting him up for a blindside. Instead, they garnered headlines worldwide for being the hardest working couple in entertainment. Following his collapse, the media portrayed Robbie as valiant in his effort to win back the young family bearing his name.

Isabel hated the Rocket twins' names. Uranus and Mercury Rocket. At least Mercury was a girl, but how did they expect a boy to live up to—much less live *with*—a name like Uranus?

Robbie thought it would make a man of his son.

Sure, *if it didn't get him killed.*

Melody's son with Hanson was named Sun. Melody Mars-Rocket never took the congressman's name as it didn't fit her persona.

The model had hired Robbie Rocket for a Hanson political fundraiser. She loved that her name worked well with a musician. Sun Mars-Hanson, his supermodel mother Melody Mars-Rocket, and his half-siblings Uranus and Mercury Rocket, were now the darlings of most American women's magazines.

The UK press was less impressed with the supermodel, but loved to skewer Robbie.

Becky came in with a tray of tea and biscuits, cubed sugar and all.

Robbie's eyes teared up. "Like mum's... Fucking fantastic."

Isabel gave Becky a nod, "I'll get Lyle."

Becky smiled as she poured a tea for Robbie and then one for herself, "I hope you don't mind if I join you for a cup."

Isabel had trained her to get details and make notes after her client chitchats, each interaction was an opportunity to get into a client's state of mind. And a chance to recognize possible public relations challenges.

Greta was convinced Judith had shared her secret with Joanne.

She grabbed a bottle of Smirnoff from the liquor store shelf, rationalizing her decision.

Vodka was easy to disguise. She often filled her water bottle for runs, but never made it to the canyon. She'd park nearby with the windows down at daybreak and drink alone.

She didn't want to die, just black out.

At first it didn't take much. She was thin and petite.

Her films were flopping and not making box office. The downward trend began with an action film that went over budget and a chase scene that killed a legendary stunt man. From there it was directors firing seasoned screenwriters and talent breaking their contracts.

That's when she became an ordained minister. She thought a higher power would fill the void and eradicate the negative thoughts that plagued her long work days on set.

It distracted her, but it didn't help her films.

Drinking helped.

She was a working drunk. A fun drunk. Her crew liked her better when she drank. It gave her a sense of humor and them the upper hand. Over time she developed a high tolerance for hard liquors.

Once a rising producer with a string of Rom-Com hits, Greta went from offers pouring in to investors no longer taking her calls.

She preferred to buy her liquor in Crenshaw, though she stood out like a sore thumb in her black Jaguar. It didn't matter, addiction was a nonjudgmental community.

She saw a man walk into the store with something shiny and black in his hand.

Was he going to rob the place?

Greta put the bottle back on the shelf and moved to get a better look. Her heart was racing. Judith would be mortified if she died in a liquor store hold up.

She could hear the man, but still couldn't see him. She ran out the door.

The man turned and ran after Greta.

She got to her car and the door was locked.

"Stay away from me!" She screamed.

He held up her clutch. "Are you looking for this?"

"Fuck," she held her chest.

"It's okay," he offered the Prada bag to her.

"Where did you find it?"

"On top of your car." He laughed, "Sorry if I scared you."

She took her purse from him, embarrassed.

"You would have figured it out when you got to the register."

She sighed. "Yeah."

She opened the bag and it seemed everything was there.

"Have a nice day," he turned and walked toward the sidewalk.

Her mind was reeling.

She grabbed a $100 bill and turned around. The man was nowhere to be seen. *Where did he go? What just happened?*

She took a deep breath, pressed the key fob in her purse and got in the car.

She understood a lot at that moment.

Judith had not told Joanne anything.

Her fear and paranoia were making her reactionary.

Poor Joanne. She hadn't been much of a friend to her today. Or to herself.

She realized this stranger had brought her to her senses. She didn't even get a chance to thank him.

If she'd bought the vodka, she'd have guzzled half the contents before she got out of the parking lot.

She started the car and began to recite the 12 steps.

CHAPTER SIX

Rick gave Joanne strict orders to stay in for the day. He had a meeting with his team. They had clients moving overseas and new corporate clients coming on board.

Joanne slept in until after 11.

She woke refreshed, ready for a quiet day to herself. She decided to lounge in her robe and pajamas. It felt good to have a leisurely breakfast and read the travel magazines she'd purchased.

She didn't read the trades, newspapers or watch television—other than shows she taped. She didn't waste time being spoon-fed the embellished news that kept viewers engaged and sponsors paying for a growing audience.

She scrutinized her living room as she sank into the sofa.

The apartment was small but well furnished. She and Zach moved in not long after she returned from Florida. He no longer wanted the big house where the media had descended on them when George found her.

Instead, they agreed to a cozy three bedroom apartment. The third bedroom started as an office but became a fitness room, so Joanne moved her desktop PC to the nook in the eat-in kitchen that had already been designed for that purpose.

Rick stayed in Jackie's old room.

Everything was luxurious. Deep cushioned sofa and chairs, plush area rugs, bamboo flooring, glass tables and artsy lamps. The kitchen office space. A compact but well-stocked chef's kitchen. Three bathrooms with showers and deep jacuzzi tubs. Nothing to want for.

She thought about her home with George and little Marquel. How very different their woodsy cabin was from this place. It was filled with hand-me-down furniture, homemade quilts, a rocking chair, a worn sofa, plaid curtains, antique dishes, plasticware, and a cast iron stove and cookware. She closed her eyes.

She could see it all again. See *them*.

Her heart quickened. She thought she'd forgotten their faces. She opened her eyes.

George moved out of a mirage before her to sit next to her on the sofa. She could hear Marquel playing.

"How are you?" He asked.

She heard him! *Was this real?*

She couldn't speak. She felt a hard knot form in her throat.

George laughed. "It's really me."

His smile was awash in a kaleidoscope of her tears. She could still see his handsome face through the blur.

She choked, "How?"

"I'm always with you." His hand went through hers.

She nodded. She understood... somehow.

"I'm sorry," she whispered.

"We are fine, Joanne. I've even made amends with your doctor husband."

She put a hand to her mouth.

"There's no place for hurt or worry. Just peace," he reassured her.

She pursed her lips and held in a sob.

George's smile was loving. "You're surrounded by love and light."

Joanne blinked away more tears and looked toward the window. A stream of sunlight burst through, dazzling in its radiance.

"Bye, mommy."

It was little Marquel's voice.

"George," Joanne turned to ask him about the light.

He was gone.

Joanne sank back as sobs wracked her body.

No one would ever believe this.

She thought about Zach.

"Zach... if you're there, be good to George and Marquel."

She yawned uncontrollably. Her cycles of anxiety were followed by excessive yawning. She decided to lay on the floor and do deep breathing exercises, trying to get control.

Still in her robe, she stretched out flat on her back. Pajama arms and legs spread out like a snow angel. Palms up. Eyes closed.

"You were here." She said it aloud, affirming it.

She began to cry uncontrollably.

"I miss you."

A feeling of euphoria was followed by engulfing sadness.

She really missed George. She couldn't even remember Zach's face at that moment, which did nothing to ebb her crying.

"Why didn't I give you a chance, George?"

She remembered the last night they were together. She had her mind made up.

"George, I want a clean start," she'd said.

He had been so hopeful.

"You're my best friend, Joanne, my only friend." His eyes welled up, "Tell me you don't love me."

"I do love you. But this love is too painful."

George got to his knees. "There was only one child in my life, and only one woman. We'll pack up and go. Now. Please... Joanne..."

She sobbed loudly. Going in and out of reality and memory.

"Please, Joanne." George grabbed her hand, "Please, I'm asking you...begging you...don't leave me."

She rocked herself through the memory, her head throbbing.

A cold chill hit her. Like a bucket of water bringing her back to now.

She was still.

"I'm all right," she said, convincing herself to sit up. She got to her knees and moved back to the sofa.

Guilt was not what George intended.

He was back in her head, showing her good times when they were young and trusting of one another. *Reminding* her.

She smiled. He was the most handsome boy in school.

She put her hand over her heart. Why couldn't she have felt this when he needed her?

Hot tears ran down her cheeks.

She then realized... It wasn't about him.

He knew that.

CHAPTER SEVEN

Marnie sat in the salon lobby looking through hairstyle books. She needed a trustworthy, yet edgy look.

"Marnie Sikes," the stylist called.

Marnie snarled, then smiled.

Still working on the new persona.

"What will we be doing for you today?" The older stylist wore her hair shaved on the left side with a comb-over of long, blonde straight tresses to the right. Her makeup appeared airbrushed. She wore black sneakers, black slacks and a black knit blouse with three quarter length sleeves. Her forearms exposed a skull tattoo. Her nails lacquered fire engine red.

Marnie thought for a moment. She didn't want to be that woman at 50. She was trying too hard.

She stood. "I need a style that screams, follow me," Marnie said plainly.

She settled into the adjustable chair, knowing the drill. The stylist would play with her hair. Try to envision her customer's wishes, match them with her ability... and hope to hell she could make Marnie happy.

"How much we taking off?" she asked.

"I want to go radically Polly-Anna. Super American Girl-next-door. Kansas wheat fields."

The hairdresser took a deep breath. "Well, we're going to have to strip out the blue. It would be best to go gradual. Your hair is damaged from over processing, I'm just being honest."

Their gazes met in the mirror while Marnie pondered the time involved in going "gradual". Time she didn't have.

"We can take several inches off, get some healthy growth coming in..."

Marnie's eyes lit up. "Shave it all off."

Her stylist took a step back, "A shaved head is not Polly-Anna, girl next door."

"No, but it skips the further damage stripping would do and takes me back to square one. Healthy hair, healthy girl."

"You sure?" This wasn't the first time a young woman sat in her chair and asked her to shave her head, but few of them went through with it. "It's the quickest route from A to B, but the regrowth stages can get awkward."

Marnie saw it as a win-win. A shaved head gave her the edge she craved, while the outgrowth would provide opportunities to try other personalities—from Manson-family to Twiggy. All good.

She shrugged, "Hell yeah. It'll grow out to my natural color and I'm back to virgin hair."

The stylist nodded. It was an easy in and out, 10 minutes tops. And the kid wasn't blinking an eye. "Okay, let's get you washed."

Rick escorted Joanne through the garage entrance of her office, avoiding the public. Her charity was one of many professions renting space in the Wilshire complex.

Joanne accepted whatever he deemed suitable for her protection, she didn't question. After all, it was his rescue of her, along with a van full of young women kidnapped by the Vasquez cartel, that gave her the resolve to do all she could to save women and children in peril.

Rick entered her office first, just as he entered all locations ahead of her to ensure her safety, then held the door for her.

Joanne walked into her office, placing her purse in a desk drawer and locking it. Another of Rick's recommendations she had adapted to, his aim was always her security. Sometimes she wondered if he remembered to take care of himself.

"See you in about an hour, Roberts is around in the meantime." He snapped his gum at her and grinned, "Don't work too hard."

"Said the man who never takes a day off," she smiled back, wondering how he made it seem so effortless.

It must get tedious, seeing the same client every day, even sharing most meals. He never complained—at least not to her—and most often his mood was agreeable. More than she could say for herself. Though she tried to be aware of her own moodswings, for his sake. Routine tasks, such as those involved with her work with the Marquel Foundation, helped keep her focused. Or at least distracted from the specters of the past.

She spent several days a week at the Foundation, studying cases and lending a hand where necessary.

The charity's staff managed the day to day fund raising operations. Joanne was a board member, and Rick an advisor as well as a law enforcement liaison. His police and government connections often helped move cases up in status.

Lou Bartalow, Zach's close friend, watched over the charity's administration. Their volunteer count increased when search operations were required, but the day to day staff of five needed little assistance. They maintained the front offices and a secured client appointment process to protect their founder and clients.

Their logo covered the wall behind her desk. A shadowy figure of a child that often reminded Joanne of a Rorschach test.

Each time she saw the logo, she saw something different. Today she saw a bird in flight.

She sat down and reviewed the photos and notes that were lined up across her desk.

Joanne greatly admired the work of *America's Most Wanted* host John Walsh.

It was his show that inspired her to start the Marquel Foundation. He was the leading media representative for Missing and

Exploited Children, aside from the newly created Amber Alert and milk cartons that pictured Missing Children.

The Marquel Foundation included missing women in their mission. Joanne was determined to give a voice to families desperately searching for their sisters, wives, daughters and mothers.

"I'm doing a perimeter check," a voice announced from the hallway.

Joanne looked up. "Hi Clark."

Clark Roberts was the foundation's official head of security. He worked for Rick and had been on detail the night Joanne was rescued.

Lou Bartalow, in his remorse for a chain of events that stemmed from his connections with Carlos Vasquez, had tabloid journalist Mark Collins sent to Bogota after the zealous reporter had wiretapped Zach Manning's house and exposed Marquel's past.

Bartalow had also hired the Jones firm to protect his deceased friend's family. The Jones team included: Jones, Clark Roberts, Bart Petty and Dane Blacksmith.

Retired Green Beret Clark Roberts successfully shot Collins in the shoulder the night the reporter held a knife to Joanne's throat.

Roberts' backup, Dane Blacksmith was a Special Ops pensioner, and Bart Petty a 20-year LAPD veteran.

"Morning Joanne," Roberts answered.

She waved him into the office.

The medium build Roberts was fair skinned and showing gray in his wheat colored tresses. He was a no nonsense guy with a task-oriented mindset.

"Rick is on a call with LAPD," Roberts reported. "Security cameras show a mystery stalker in the stairwell leading to our floor."

Joanne was surprised. "How do you know it's a stalker?"

"An employee or volunteer wouldn't hide in the stairwell or alleyway near the parking garage when they could walk through the front door. It's possible that it's unrelated to the foundation. Could be someone watching one of our neighbors."

"Does it ever end?" Joanne was disappointed.

"We'll see to it." Roberts affirmed.

She appreciated his confidence. "I'm sure."

"On that note," Roberts started to leave.

Joanne looked at the array of files and photos on her desk. "Could the stalker be associated with one of these newer cases?"

Roberts was moving out of the office and into the hallway. "Don't know. Hope to get a better look at the footage. See if we can identify the guy."

"How do you know it's a guy?" Joanne stood, calling out.

"Suspicious person," he corrected himself as he moved down the hall.

Joanne caught up with him.

Clark paused, "Did I miss something?"

Joanne shook her head.

He waited for Joanne to pass.

She stopped, staring at him. "I'm going with you."

"With?"

"How else am I going to learn?" Joanne was serious.

He took a deep breath and resumed walking briskly.

"I'm tired of being a victim." She meant it.

"That's the spirit," Roberts knew who signed his check.

CHAPTER EIGHT

J udith put her book down. "I've been thinking."
The short-statured doctor looked like a child in the king size
bed. She was freshly showered. Her salt and pepper tresses glistened with dampness, her horn-rimmed glasses perched on the
bridge of her nose.

Greta poked her head out of the bathroom. Toothpaste foamed
from her mouth. She kept brushing, returning to the sink.

Judith smiled, "Let's have Ken and Evan over for a barbecue.
We'll invite Joanne, Rick, Jackie and Josh, too."

Greta spit. "We're vegetarian, Judith."

Judith's tone became apologetic. "I've had meat in the last
few weeks—at lunch. It tasted delicious."

"I'm not eating flesh." Greta scrubbed her back teeth furiously. The thought of putting meat in her mouth made her want
to gag.

"It doesn't seem to bother you when we dine with others,"
Judith pointed out, though she knew she was on shaky ground
with this idea.

Greta spit again. "Are you straight, too? Have you had some
dick in the last few weeks that I should know about?"

Judith laughed heartily. "No."

"Then what gives?" Greta stared at her clean face in the mirror, feeling less guilty about her near relapse with the bottle. She
rinsed her mouth and turned out the bathroom light.

Judith pat the bed beside her. "Greta, darling. I'm reading this book... they are having the best time. They've moved their kitchen outdoors and their dining room set is on the lawn and it just sounds charming."

"Then we'll serve salads, veggie casseroles, fruits and cheese..."

Judith handed Greta her book. "Read that and tell me you don't want to try barbecue."

Greta obliged her partner and read the paragraph.

"I don't want barbecue." Greta returned the book.

"Fine." Judith secured her page and closed the book, placing it on her nightstand.

Greta pounded and fluffed her pillows before pulling the sheets back and sliding in next to Judith. "We can still have everyone over..." Greta agreed. "Maybe invite a few new faces, to break up the sameness of our conversations."

"Hire some extras?" Judith laughed.

Greta gave Judith a kiss. "I'll put out a casting call."

"Wouldn't it be fun?" Judith was genuinely excited.

Greta grabbed a script from her bedside table and a set of readers from a basket of pens and post it notes. "But we're not serving meat, Judith. I'm trying my best to stay..." she trailed off as she scanned the screenplay.

"Sober," Judith finished her sentence.

"Healthy. Healthy is what I was going for. Why did you say sober?" Greta threw her hand up. "We're talking about meat, for Christ's sake."

"I'm sorry, darling. You're in recovery. Which means we're both in recovery," Judith reached for Greta's hand.

Greta pulled away. "Alcohol is the answer to all of my prob-lems, Dr. Wright. I think of alcohol 24/7. I really do, but that's beside the point. I feel you don't trust me and I hate it!"

Judith listened, knowing not to push her lover while she was venting.

"I'm sensitive, okay?" Greta couldn't look at Judith. "And perhaps I want you to feel bad for your comment. AND eating meat! But damn it, Judith, I'm scared."

"Scared of what?" Judith asked. She wanted Greta to process her fear.

"I'm afraid I'll fuck up the next film I get. That the curse will continue. A string of failures." Greta held her breath. She didn't want to break down.

Judith stroked Greta's long blonde hair.

"Greta, your best *is* good enough. Let the universe handle the rest."

"The universe hates me," Greta sobbed.

"I'm your biggest fan, Greta darling."

"I don't want to let you down," she rubbed her eyes. She didn't want Judith to know how close she came to letting addiction win.

"I'm not going to eat meat," Judith decided. "I don't want to disturb your Chi."

"That would make me happy." Greta smiled.

"I'll go to Barbecue Anonymous, should I ever slip again," Judith laughed.

Greta sighed. "That reminds me. I abandoned Joanne at brunch the other day. I knew Rick was watching her, so I didn't bother to apologize or follow up."

"Oh," Judith was surprised.

Greta grabbed a tissue from the bedside table and blew her nose.

"What happened?" Judith couldn't imagine. Greta always returned from visits with Joanne seeming refreshed.

"Are you concerned for Joanne or me?" Greta asked. "You look terribly unhappy."

"It doesn't sound like you. Which makes me wonder what Joanne did? Should I be concerned?"

Greta took a few deep breaths. "Joanne did nothing. I took something she said out of context. I thought you told her I was back at AA."

Judith thought for a moment. "I wouldn't share our private struggles with Joanne, she is a patient who happens to be a friend... but still a patient. And you aren't *back* in AA, you'll always be in AA. It's your support system..."

Greta stopped Judith, "I tried to buy vodka after I left Joanne. I know it was the addiction pushing me. I wanted to believe it was you or Joanne that did something to justify my anger. As it turns out, I left my purse on top of the car."

"Your purse?" Judith didn't follow. "Did you lose it?"

Greta paused. "I lost it, all right. I thought someone was trying to rob the liquor store..."

"What on earth?" Judith was uncertain where Greta's story was going.

Greta started to cry again. "I thought the guy trying to return my handbag wanted to rob the store... or come after me."

Judith stopped Greta from saying any more. "You got your purse back, then?"

Greta nodded.

Judith continued, "And you got through it, you didn't drink. You stayed sober."

Greta agreed and sobbed. "You can eat barbecue if you want."

Judith stifled a laugh, "No. I'll find another book to read and we'll hold off entertaining for a bit."

Greta kissed Judith's hand. "I need to apologize to Joanne."

Judith removed her glasses and leaned in for a goodnight kiss.

Greta kissed her lover and hugged her tight.

Judith returned the embrace, squeezing Greta reassuringly.

"I'm sure Joanne will be understanding," Judith released Greta and positioned her pillows for sleep.

"I love you," Greta said.

"I love you more," Judith replied.

Greta picked up her script and opened it to a marked page.

Judith turned to face away from the light.

Greta didn't know what she'd ever do without Judith. Her lover always gave her a reason to believe in herself.

Ken buttered a few slices of toast while Evan scrambled their eggs.

"I'm meeting Jackie at FieldHause," Evan said over his shoulder. "We're going to look at some fabrics. I'm considering having the chaise restuffed and recovered."

Ken stepped closer to him, his face screwed up in suspicion.

Evan slapped him on the ass. "That is not an attractive expression."

"I'm not buying it," Ken said. "You always buy new. You're up to something."

Evan laughed. "I'm trying to help Jackie."

"Since when does she need help?" Ken moved the plate of toast to the already set table, where they had a selection of bacon, fruit, cheese and jams.

"I'm being a friend. Is that okay?" Evan placed eggs on both of their plates.

They sat.

"I'll find out," Ken assured Evan.

"Yes, you will," Evan said, "but for now that's all I'm saying."

Ken's mouth dropped.

Evan grabbed the toast and layered eggs, cream cheese, bacon and a touch of peppered jelly on it, creating a hearty sandwich.

"You should slice your sandwich," Ken muttered.

Evan focused on the task of eating and not talking with his mouth full. Ken always blurted what was on his mind.

"Give me a bite?" Ken asked.

Evan held the sandwich out while Ken took a big bite and immediately started talking through his chewing.

"What's the big secret?"

Evan cut the remaining sandwich in half and gave Ken a portion. It seemed he could never get through a meal without giving Ken half.

If he made the same sandwich for Ken to begin with, it was never as appealing.

"Ken," was Evan's only response, aside from slicing an orange into thin layers and pairing it with brie and a cracker.

Ken was like a cat, following Evan's every move. "I thought you liked berries with brie."

Evan continued to eat.

"Is it good?" Ken wanted a bite.

Evan made the same combination again and fed Ken.

"Does she get a commission?" Ken asked as soon as the food was in his mouth.

Evan pushed the plunger down on the French press as he poured Ken half a cup, then himself a full cup. Ken liked his coffee sweet and Evan left him room for plenty of sugar and cream. "It's just our girl time."

"Why didn't you say that," Ken shook his head, "instead of acting like you're planning something without me?"

Ken milked down his coffee and began shoveling sugar in.

Evan watched his lover fill his cup to brimming. He handed Ken a cinnamon stick and a added a splash of pure vanilla before he could ask.

Ken stirred the mixture with the cinnamon stick.

"I need a girl day, too," he complained. "Maybe Josh and I can grab pedicures and brunch."

He slurped his coffee.

Evan knew what was coming next.

"It's cold, Ev," Ken handed Evan his cup.

"Next time we'll warm the creamer," Evan got up to microwave Ken's coffee.

"We always say that and you forget," Ken grabbed a slice of bacon and began munching.

Evan waited by the microwave while Ken rambled on about the best places he could get a pedicure—and not a case of toenail fungus—until it beeped twice. He placed the hot cup in front of Ken and seated himself again.

"I'll be lucky if I can sip it in the next hour," Ken blew on the steam.

Evan poured a third of Ken's coffee into his cup and returned it with an additional shot of cream.

Ken slurped and smiled. "Perfect."

Evan adored Ken's quirks. "I love you."

"Get over here and prove it," Ken batted his eyes.

Evan reached for Ken's thigh.

Ken slapped his hand. "A girl wants to finish her beverage."

Evan turned his chair and pulled Ken's up between his long legs.

"Patience is a virtue," Ken teased.

"We'll see how much patience you have..."

Evan held Ken's gaze while his hands traveled down to unbuckle his belt.

CHAPTER NINE

Humberto sat on the bleachers watching the other inmates shoot hoops.

He and his fellow residents at California State Prison at Corcoran were notorious criminals. Their crimes ranged from murder, attempted murder, voluntary manslaughter, robbery, to kidnapping and drug trafficking—on the short list.

The compound of sprawling buildings focused on offender type, inmate programs, hospital facilities, guard towers, secure holding facilities known as SHU or isolation cells, substance abuse programs and administration.

Better known as COR to law enforcement, the property stretched out in an imperfect circle that could easily be mistaken for an extraterrestrial landing pad. The perimeter of specialized fence, electronic detection and rolls of razor wire promised to keep the animals in and the protestors out.

Sirhan Sirhan, Charles Manson, members of the Mexican mafia and now he, leader of the Vasquez cartel, all kept company at COR.

The general population didn't commune with the celebrity criminals Sirhan and Manson. They had handlers, guards who oversaw their stay. Not that they didn't have brushes with the universe inside, but exposure was limited.

Brutality by corrections officers was understood as a casualty of war. It varied with management changes, inmate changes, staff attrition and acceptance.

Good guys vs. bad guys.

The lines were blurring as the good guys (AKA corrections officers) often used unlawful action against the bad guys (AKA inmates).

Humberto's people kept officer Jeremiah Wakes family handsomely fed and housed. This was one way to secure his safety inside.

Humberto's team was losing the basketball game.

An inmate sat next to him on the bleacher. "Gallo is on to your telenovela fixation."

Humberto had nothing to hide. He was a proud man. He wasn't in COR because he lacked passion.

"How about some pancakes," Humberto shouted to Wakes, The solid 6'7", 300 lb guard watched the game as he walked through. He ignored the Colombian.

The opposing team passed the ball to Humberto's team. They tied the game.

Fifty percent of the population was in for life, if they had their life.

Everyone knew you couldn't make pancakes without batter. Most would rather lose than be battered by Humberto's thugs.

Humberto left the bleachers and greeted one of his gang members. They exchanged a hug and contraband and continued in a heated discussion.

CHAPTER TEN

Jackie and Josh spied Isabel and Lyle across the crowded restaurant and began making their way to the horseshoe shaped booth. They could both see and be seen, which didn't thrill Jackie.

Josh shook Lyle's hand while Jackie slid into the booth alongside Isabel.

Josh was hungry. He'd just finished a double shift and was ready to eat, go home and sleep.

Isabel pushed the basket of bread over to him.

"It's that obvious," he yawned. He didn't even bother to butter his bread.

"Was traffic bad?" Isabel was perturbed. They had waited almost an hour and Lyle was on his third martini. She didn't mind him drinking when they were home, but one of them had to maintain composure.

"When isn't traffic bad? Josh had a patient who needed stitches at the last minute," Jackie elbowed Josh, who was beginning to nod off.

Lyle spotted Melody Mars by the bar and excused himself.

Isabel waved to Melody, but the younger woman didn't see her.

Isabel turned to Jackie, "I can order for Lyle." She pushed menus toward Jackie and Josh.

Jackie glanced over the top of her menu. "Mother, Lyle is touching Melody's ass."

Isabel looked over and saw Lyle with his arm around the model's waist. "He's handling her PR, not her ass. You're mistaken. I'm looking right at them."

Jackie shrugged.

Josh put his head on Jackie's shoulder, closing his eyes. "Order me anything and wake me when it's served."

Isabel remembered a time when she and Zach were in college. They were very much like Jackie and Josh. Zach was dedicated to his studies and looking forward to private practice.

Isabel motioned a waiter over and ordered lobster tails for herself and Lyle. Jackie and Josh were having steaks. By the time they had the details ironed out, Lyle had returned.

"What's so urgent with Melody," Isabel asked Lyle.

"She wants to pose nude, show her nipples to the world," Lyle announced.

"They're fine. She didn't suffer any permanent damage..." Isabel was not following.

Josh sat up, blinking. "A publicity stunt to boost her bras... her bra company."

Jackie was not expecting this reaction from him.

Lyle pointed to Josh in agreement, then slugged the rest of his martini. "She's going to have an enlargement as part of her... reconstruction and emotional recovery."

Jackie balked. "To pose nude?"

"Shh," Lyle hiccuped. "Advance publicity has to be carefully timed."

Jackie's voice was lower, "I'm not buying a bra because a supermodel had a breast enlargement and posed nude."

Lyle pointed to Josh again.

Josh obliged. "Men will see her nude centerfold and buy her brand when gift shopping for their wives. She's selling a transformation fantasy."

Isabel and Jackie both stared at Josh.

He shrugged, "I minored in marketing."

Lyle stifled a burp, "Really? Why?"

"I like Superbowl commercials. Thought it would be a good backup plan." Josh noshed on more bread.

Isabel shook her head and excused herself.

Jackie listened to the men go on briefly, then elected to excuse herself as well.

Isabel was seated in front of the mirror in the powder room when Jackie walked in.

Their eyes met in the mirror.

"I'm finally beginning to understand your father," Isabel sighed.

Jackie sat next to her mother, unsure where this revelation was coming from.

She put her hand on Isabel's. "Really, mother?"

She nodded.

"I wish I could tell him," Isabel's hand trembled in Jackie's grip.

Jackie rubbed her mother's hand. "You can talk to him. I do."

Isabel smiled, her eyes watering. "Joanne got the best of him."

They stared at their reflections.

"He married you first," Jackie offered. She felt oddly closer to her mother in this moment than she ever had. "He fell in love with you and you both had me."

Isabel grabbed a tissue. "He tried to convince me. But I was so enamored by Hollywood. I never listened.—I'm sure Lyle loves me." Her laugh was bitter, "We deserve each other."

"Are you concerned because I mentioned he was touching Melody's ass?" Jackie now regretted saying anything.

Isabel dabbed her tears. "I'm not complaining. We work well together and I'm lucky to be married. He's a power player. He could start a family with a woman your age."

Jackie grimaced.

Isabel laughed. "There are plenty of starlets and models looking for a meal ticket."

A toilet flushed.

They both fell silent, having thought they were alone.

"Hi Isabel," Melody stumbled out of the stall to the wash basin. Her dress was so short her cheeks peeked out as she grabbed at the sink. Her evening bag fell from her hand to the floor as her oversized bracelets followed.

Jackie pointed Isabel's attention to the trail of toilet tissue dragging behind the model.

Ever the businesswoman, Isabel stood and smiled. "Let's help you, dear."

Melody couldn't seem to steady herself in her heels.

Isabel could smell vomit. She wasn't certain if Melody was purging, super drunk, or just sick.

Jackie got up as well, stepping on the string of tissue on the highly polished black floor. It broke, but a few feet remained dangling from Melody's rear.

"Ms. Mars," Jackie was polite, "you have... tissue hanging."

Melody attempted to steady herself again, turning her back to the mirror and pulling her dress up. She had nothing on underneath. Her perfectly shaped ass gripped several squares of toilet paper between her cheeks, as she peered over her shoulder, assessing.

"Jesus, I can't feel a thing." She grabbed at the paper, wobbling on her stiletto heels, and the dress dropped back into place.

Isabel seized a cotton wash cloth the restaurant supplied for their patrons' hands.

"Hold still," Isabel lifted Melody's dress and wiped the model's ass. She then threw the tissue and cloth in the trash.

Jackie was both disturbed and impressed. She picked up Melody's handbag and bracelets and placed them on the basin shelf.

Isabel encouraged Melody to freshen up.

"I heard you," Melody splashed her face. Isabel handed her a small cup of mouthwash from a dispenser.

Melody gargled, spit, then rubbed her face with a dry wash cloth. Her skin radiated pink, like she'd just stepped off the runway or from a soap commercial shoot.

"How do you do that?" Jackie was amazed. "Your skin is beautiful."

Melody shrugged. "Facials?"

"I apologize," Isabel said to Melody, "if I offended you."

"No, I apologize," Jackie clarified. "I thought I saw Lyle put his hand on your..."

"Ass," Melody finished.

Jackie sighed. "Yes, that's what I said."

Melody picked up her purse and bracelets and moved toward the vanity. "I guess we're even. Isabel had her hand on my ass, too, so all's well that ends well," she sat.

Literally, Isabel thought.

Jackie wouldn't let it go. "But really. Did he have his hand on your ass?"

Isabel turned her back to Melody so she could glare at Jackie.

"Likely," Melody said. "It's not the first time. They all do it."

Isabel sat next to Melody.

"Why do you put up with it?" Jackie asked.

"Put up with what?" Melody looked confused.

Isabel wasn't about to interrupt the conversation. Jackie remained quiet, awaiting Melody's answer.

Melody laughed, "It's my *ass*et." She put on some melon colored lipstick and ran her fingers through her hair, then slipped her bracelets back on. "My mother raised me to believe your body is a tool. Let a man touch you and you control him."

"What did your father say?" Jackie was shocked. "What about your husband?'

Melody was applying fresh eyeliner.

"Never met my dad," she was frank. "Mother's been an alcoholic her entire life. Likely never knew who fucked her or if she consented. I love her. Can't change her—I don't want Mercury to be like me. I'd rather she be more like you..." Melody looked at Jackie in the mirror. "As for Robbie, he's busy grabbing asses. It's all we know. Celebrity is a sick existence. No one should *want* to be us. Am I right, Isabel?"

Isabel said nothing.

Melody was smart... and a client.

"I don't," Jackie said. "No offense."

"Stay that way," Melody stood, transformed. Ready for the spotlight. She smiled several times in the mirror, checking her teeth, then pulled her dress down again. "I'm sure the tide will turn someday, but until then, business as usual." She held her right hand up and twirled her bejeweled wrist as she catwalked out of the restroom. "Carry on, ladies."

The door closed behind her and the dining room noise disappeared with it, leaving mother and daughter in a pregnant silence.

Jackie turned to her mother, "That wash cloth you used on Melody's ass is a scrapbook treasure for someone."

Isabel laughed. "Yours was the last ass I wiped that wasn't my own—until today."

"I was wondering about that..." Jackie put her arm around her mother's shoulder. "Ass wiper."

CHAPTER ELEVEN

Joanne picked up the phone on the second ring, "Manning residence."

The caller's voice was super bubbly, "Hi Joanne, it's Marnie."

"Marnie?" Joanne was surprised. "Are you looking for Jackie?"

Marnie laughed. "I'm not."

Joanne was more surprised. "How can I help you?"

Rick was in the other room.

Something about Marnie's voice didn't sound right to Joanne.

"I'd like to volunteer for your charity."

"I'm sorry, Marnie," Joanne didn't hesitate, knowing she had to be clear. "You were caught breaking into Isabel's house..."

Marnie's laugh interrupted her, "That was just a phase. I'm not that kid anymore and I'm an adult now. Surely you can forgive me?"

Rick walked in, noting Joanne's discomfort with the caller.

"Hold, please." Joanne covered the receiver.

"Who is it?" Rick wanted to know.

"Marnie Sikes."

"The Manson-family wannabe?" Rick was clearly suspicious. "I'll get a trace."

Joanne shook her head. "She wants to volunteer at the foundation, said she's changed."

Rick snapped his gum. His jaw pulsed, "She's working you."

Joanne took a deep breath, considering. "I've changed. Maybe she has?"

"Not debating with you," Rick chewed faster.

"I'd like to believe the best in others," Joanne held the phone against her stomach.

"No bullshit, Joanne. That kid is trouble." He was firm. He knew her impulse was to forgive, but his neck hairs were up and she had to be reined in.

"I know," Joanne said. The phone was pressing into the scar that had long ago healed. The scar caused by another troubled young person, Adrian Dane Jackson—a memorabilia collector who shot Joanne at a public speaking engagement. She shuddered.

"Her background check won't fly," he tried to direct her thoughts with the facts of the situation. "You say you want to stay out of the media and off the radar—bringing that Sikes freak into the foundation is a media bonbon."

That did the trick, he could tell. Rick sighed and rubbed his forehead, relieved.

Joanne returned to the call. "Are you still there, Marnie?"

There was a pause, "Hey, it sounds like you're busy. Sorry, I interrupted."

Joanne thought she heard sincerity in the apology. Then Marnie hung up.

She turned to Rick. "Zach always said Marnie's parents gave her too much freedom. He would have been mortified by her actions."

Jones nodded agreement.

She couldn't help feeling the girl deserved a second chance. "I've never even met Marnie in person, it seems wrong to write her off entirely."

Rick didn't believe in coincidence. "This is the first time she's called? How did she get your phone number?"

"She could have called Jackie here before," Joanne shrugged. "Can't we believe she's grown up? That she wants to do good?"

"No," Rick was blunt. "Joanne, I'm here to protect you. Feel free to maintain your optimism, but it's my job to find out what Marnie Sikes is up to. I've got calls to make."

A photographer's vehicle inched closer and clicked a few photos of Joanne leaving the apartment with Rick. The couple was heading south.

Joanne's building security guard waved a fist at the photographer. "No paparazzi!"

The photographer shot the guard a bird. "Free country."

The unmarked car sped away as the guard scrambled to jot down a description.

Evan greeted Jackie with a basket of spring flowers.

"Congrats," he gave her a big hug.

Jackie beamed. "You are the *only* one who knows, other than Josh."

She gestured for him to sit as she placed the basket on her desk.

"Josh will likely cave soon and start 'trusting' his colleagues. Asking them not to repeat that we're engaged."

They were alone in the warehouse.

Evan sat on a stool behind the production counter, his long legs reached the floor. "Ken would. Who are we kidding? He would have agreed to keep it a secret, then tell everyone he made eye contact with and beg them not to tell me."

Jackie laughed, "That's our Ken. Thankfully he has you."

"Thankfully we have each other, just as you and Josh do." Evan looked well. His dark hair was grown out just a bit longer than usual and he wore a healthy tan, along with khaki shorts, a neutral toned Hawaiian shirt and sandals. "Have you chosen colors?"

Jackie placed a few swatches on the work table. Her navy FH production apron hid her floral sundress.

"I'm not sure, yet." Jackie added some paint cards. "I've seen some combinations of purple, aqua and tangerine."

Evan knew how much she wanted sincere guidance. He wasn't certain he could get behind this pallet.

"What speaks to you?" Evan put his glasses on and looked at the samples, feeling the swatches.

Jackie thumbed through some bridal magazines and pointed out some suits and ties. "I don't have any friends that could be bridesmaids, other than Joanne. I was thinking you, Joanne and Ken might be my bridesmaids. Josh has a few doctor buddies to be his groomsmen."

Evan stared at her. Her soft brown-blonde hair was twisted up in a knot, which was a simple, classic look. Unfazed by the invitation to be a bridesmaid, he fought the urge to steer her away from the color combination she had threatened him with—he would wait and see where things led.

"Your hair looks great like that, by the way," he offered. "A simple up-do might be nice for the ceremony."

It was as though her father were looking through him.

She laughed, "I wasn't listening."

"I'm aware." He smiled. "What do these colors mean to you?"

Jackie picked up the purple and her voice became quiet. "This represents my dad. Purple is majestic and spiritual. I miss him. I wish he could be here. I originally thought Lyle would walk me down the aisle, but I'm going to ask my mother. I'm not sure I respect him. Mother and I are actually getting closer..."

Evan understood. "What about Josh's family?"

"Okay, full disclosure: his is not a happy story. He was raised by his grandmother. His parents were both in the military. His dad was killed in a helicopter crash. His mother was a nurse—kind of why he's in medicine. She had a biopsy at a military hospital and they nicked one of her internal organs. She bled to death internally." She paused for a moment, closing her eyes. "And his grandmother isn't doing well. She's in a nursing home."

Evan had not heard any of this before. "He has an amazing disposition, given what he's gone through."

Jackie put the bridal magazine aside. "When we met, he thought Joanne was my mother. He couldn't believe I had both parents struggling for their lives on two different floors of the hospital."

Evan sat up straighter and crossed his arms. This made sense, "He understood exactly what you were going through. No wonder he was drawn to you."

Jackie nodded, her voice breaking, "Sometimes tragedy creates a beautiful bond."

Evan didn't want her to dwell on sadness. He placed his right hand on the color swatches.

"Josh is okay with these colors?"

"He's totally fine with anything. He just wants to get through it." She put the purple aside. "I love tangerine. It is so vibrant, it just makes me smile. It's a fun color and I want to start our lives together having fun. We need joy before we start making babies. *Lots* of joy."

"I think there is a lot of joy in making babies," Evan winked.

Jackie blushed. "You sound just like my dad! In fact, I feel you're channeling him."

"I wouldn't mind if I was," Evan studied the blue card. "What about turquoise?"

Jackie walked over to the coffee maker and began scooping the FH favorite blend into a filter. "I really didn't think of it as turquoise so much as kind of a seafoam or teal."

"Seafoam is grayish-white," Evan peered over his frames.

"Not real seafoam, the color." Jackie clarified as she poured water in the coffeemaker. "I find it tranquil."

"What if you incorporate real turquoise in stone form? Perhaps some accent for Josh... A bolo tie? Or even for the groomsmen?"

Jackie laughed. "Josh would love that! But he'd want some cowboy looking thing. He's kind of flamboyant when it comes to showing off to his doctor friends."

"My kind of guy," Evan smiled. "Where will the ceremony be?"

"Malibu, we're hoping. Nothing fancy, just on the beach. Sunset." Jackie closed her eyes. "I see us all semi-formal... and semi-casual. But not *too* semi-casual."

The aroma of coffee permeated their immediate surroundings. A cozy, comfortable feeling embraced Jackie.

Evan closed his eyes, too. "Turquoise. The ocean." He nodded, deciding. "Tangerine is the setting sun and nightfall your purple."

Jackie opened her eyes, her smile radiant. "Yes!"

"I believe turquoise was originally called Turkish stone." Evan cut a chunk of the paint card and taped it to his shirt. "All gems and stones have energy. You should look it up. What do you think?"

Jackie examined the color against his print shirt.

"Too busy." She took it off of him and stuck it to her apron.

"Nice contrast with the navy," Evan approved. "What color for Josh's tuxedo?

"White. Since we'll be outdoors. Should it be a tux? Can you think of an alternative?" She poured Evan a black coffee and placed it on the counter.

"That depends on your dress," Evan pushed the glasses down on his nose. She certainly had no shortage of ideas. He was ready to suggest an elimination process, but he waited.

"I'm thinking of a ballet cut." Jackie picked up the bridal magazine again to find an example. "Oh, or a mermaid gown," she pointed to a photo.

Evan was non-committal. "So... music box ballerina or Disney's Little Mermaid?"

"Music box ballerina sounds adorable," Jackie liked it. "But mermaid sounds beachy."

This was going to be more work than he thought. At least he knew she really needed his advice, she wasn't just asking to make him feel involved. "The ballerina dress might be more comfortable. It wouldn't sweep the sand."

"True, but the mermaid might be cute," Jackie was torn.

"So it is a beach theme?" Evan pushed his glasses up into his hair.

"That's what you're here for. We're figuring that out."

"Can we go back to something you said earlier?" Evan sipped his coffee.

Jackie poured cream into her coffee and sat down, stirring it with a long spoon.

"You said you didn't have bridesmaids. While I'm flattered, and I'm happy to be a bride's man... Don't you have any friends from college or high school you'd like to consider?"

"Marnie was my best friend, but you know how that turned out. I haven't spoken to her in forever... And even if I did, GOD no!" She wrapped both hands around her mug, becoming pensive. "When I met Josh, I just stopped hanging out with classmates. Plus, there was the Marquel/Joanne stories in the press. I couldn't trust anyone. You and Ken are my best friends. Well, there is Aunt Sophie..."

"Gala gal Sophie Krentz?" Evan laughed. "She could be your Ursula if you go with the mermaid theme."

Jackie laughed. "That was mean."

"My inner bitch, sorry." Evan took another gulp of coffee, "Plenty of charities benefit from her efforts, but her guests often end up tabloid fodder. She likes to pit adversaries—as you know. Maybe not the best energy for a wedding party."

"She's not really my aunt," Jackie clarified. "She's mom's college roommate."

Evan shook his head. "Jackie you are too young to have all these old people in your wedding party."

Jackie laughed. "You're not old. You're just right."

He reached over and touched her nose. "Hey Goldilocks, I have news for you. Baby Bear had all the goods. Age appropriate for Goldilocks. Which pretty much sums up my point."

"I don't care."

Evan stood to stretch. He had to get her someplace where she could see the reality of her ideas in living color. "Can we take this meeting to a bridal shop or a department store? Shouldn't we be gasping over gaudy china patterns or trying on veils?"

Jackie brightened up. "I'll get my purse."

"Let's go to Glendale. I've friends who can help," Evan finished his coffee.

She took off her apron and went to shut down the computer. "Wait, I'm going to look up the meaning of turquoise really quick." She pulled up the Infoseek page and typed.

Evan came around the table, putting his glasses back on.

They both read: Turquoise—a sacred stone, healing, provides protection and integrity for the wearer.

Evan liked it. "I think Zach would want the whole wedding party to wear turquoise. In stone form," he emphasized.

Jackie shut the computer down. "He'd likely say mother and Lyle could use the integrity. But you're right. He'd love it."

She looped her arm through Evan's. "You should walk me down the aisle."

"While I'm honored, your mother was a great suggestion." Evan patted her arm, "I'll be standing beside you in a seafoam tuxedo, tangerine cummerbund and purple bow tie."

"That's disgusting. Seriously!" She elbowed him. "I have good taste—You'll see."

CHAPTER TWELVE

"Man down." The LAPD officer radioed to his dispatch. The radio scratched a reply.

Rick Jones was listening with his police scanner. Joanne was napping in the other room.

He kept the scanner on low. He wanted to be aware of any unusual activity in the area. Anything out of the norm.

Nothing related developed.

He moved to the living room with his Gateway laptop. He wanted to compile the intel on Marnie Sikes.

Joanne was curled up on the couch.

Rick moved to the kitchen table. He saw her stirring. At first, he thought she was waking, then realized she must be dreaming.

His gaze kept returning to her sleeping form while he waited for the laptop to start up.

There was a tickling in his solar plexus as he remembered her impulse to forgive Marnie Sikes. He knew it was based on what Joanne considered to be her own past mistakes. How could he convince her that she was a victim of PTSD, her own fears of loss and abandonment, even of the Hollywood machine? He couldn't remember ever seeing her misstep or act selfishly, surely she didn't deserve the bowl of crap life had handed her.

His jaw tightening, he reminded himself he was there as a professional. He may want to crawl onto the sofa beside her and wrap himself around her, make the world the kind of place that deserved a woman like Joanne Manning. Never let anything bad happen to her again, but that wasn't the way the world worked.

That didn't change the fact that if he could do all those things—for her—he would.

Joanne sat next to George. She'd been in this dream before. They were in a dark honky-tonk. Garth Brooks' *The Dance* began to play.

She grabbed the beer that he had waiting for her and took a swig.

It was warm. She could barely swallow it.

"It's been sitting awhile," he said.

George had a collection of empties in front of him and one full beer sitting there for Joanne.

She held out her hand.

"Dance with me," she said.

George's eyes were red. He was thin. Not the George she last saw.

Tears spilled. He followed her.

The song came to the line '*all the world was right.*'

He broke down and held her tight. They barely moved.

She tried to dance, but he wouldn't follow.

The weight of him morphed into a darkness where she went into a house.

Their house.

The cabin in the woods.

She saw new rooms. Additions.

Their old furnishings looked new.

She looked for George and saw a baby.

The baby was on the floor and she couldn't pick it up.

Rick appeared. He reached his hand out to her.

Why was he in their house?

She ran outside looking for George. She couldn't figure out how to get back to the bar. She wanted to return to George's embrace.

The song was back.

George sang along as he faded out, '...better left to chance.'

Greta listened to the young director.

He wore an oversized baseball cap backwards, a white tee, acid-wash jeans and Air Jordans. His tangled curls appeared as alfalfa sprouts spewing from the edges of his hat. He was smart, privileged, and knew it.

He needed a budget. He had most of his funds secured.

She felt good.

He loved her early hits—he wanted a producer who could teach him the business.

The script was solid. A Rom-Com with a name actor which promised international distribution. This could be her comeback.

They had worked out the contract arrangements by phone earlier, but she wanted a face-to-face. A better understanding of his vision before she signed.

Today felt like a new beginning...

It had been a long time coming.

The director had waited for her at a pub table near the bar. Not her preference, but she figured it was good to be out of her comfort zone.

He had a lot to say, but she had yet to get a feel for his ability. She waited for him to take a breath, then joined his conversation.

"What do you see as the tone of the film?" She took off her jacket and put in on the chair back, placing the contract on the table.

His cell rang.

Hers was on silent.

He took the call.

She kept a smile on her face. She waited. She listened. It didn't sound like a call that needed to disrupt their meeting.

She thought about her other films... about the things that started her on the path of drinking. Why did she let failure get to her?

She wasn't a bad person. She loved her work. She could help newcomers like this young man. So, what if a stunt man died? It was an accident. Stunt people take chances. That wasn't sloppy. They had insurance.

Okay, they went over budget. Who *doesn't* go over budget?

The director continued making weekend plans with the caller. She watched his confidence. She remembered what that felt like.

The waitress came over and placed two bloody marys in front of the director and a glass of water in front of Greta.

"What would you like, hon?" The waitress asked.

"A sparkling water would be great," Greta's smile was sincere. It really felt great to be back in the business.

The director mumbled to her, "two for one."

He kept talking into his phone and pushed one of the drinks in front of Greta.

She stared at it until the waitress brought her sparkling water in a glass bottle and a cold tumbler with ice.

Greta opened her water and took a swig, still eying the bloody mary. Tasting it in her mind.

The director watched her as he kept talking.

"Hey," he said. "I gotta go."

Greta was still focused on the drink.

"Did I do something wrong, like we don't drink at meetings?" He was uncertain.

He waved the waitress over, not waiting for Greta's reply. "I'll have a diet soda. Just take these away. I'll pay for them."

Greta smiled again. It was her way of avoiding conflict.

The director smiled back. "Are you still going to work with me?"

His phone rang again and he put it on silent.

"I don't drink. I'm a recovering alcoholic," Greta said. "I don't mind what you do in your off hours, but when we're working, you and I don't drink."

She could feel her resolve growing stronger.

"That's cool." He nodded.

"Who were you talking to?" Greta felt a hint of confidence returning.

"That was our backer. He's having a party this weekend at Big Bear. He wants me to meet some people he's bringing. They might want to invest."

Greta drummed her fingers on the tabletop. "How many points are we talking?"

"Not sure. Maybe two?"

Greta was concerned. "Depending on the number of investors, it could get murky trying to control expectations—if everyone has an opinion."

The waitress placed his diet soda on the table.

He took a sip. "That reminds me, the main backer has a few family members who would like to audition. I didn't promise anything."

Greta took a deep breath. "Do they act?"

"Not sure."

"Can I give you some advice?" She truly hoped he would say yes.

"Absolutely."

"Don't go to Big Bear. But if you do, don't partake of whatever pleasures might be at your disposal. You want to be an observer." Greta straightened her posture. She wanted him to succeed and survive. "The parties will only get bigger. Look to your idols. The craftsmen and craftswomen who make tent-poles year in and year out..."

He held up his hand. "That's not going to work. The money came from one of these events. These dudes are fucked up, rich and bored."

Greta felt bile rise in her throat. "You owe me for the budget. I'm going to have to pass." She tore the contract in half.

"How is that fair? If you hadn't been eavesdropping... you wouldn't have known. Don't be a bitch."

Greta got up.

"That would have come out eventually." She threw a twenty on the table.

Joanne hugged Judith. They went into Judith's office.

"It's been awhile." Joanne sat down.

Judith sat across from Joanne in her red leather Queen Anne office chair. It had been custom built for her short stature, so her feet could reach the floor.

"Greta and I were just talking about you." Judith grabbed her pen and pad. "We're thinking of hosting a get together and having you and Rick, Josh, Jackie, Ken and Evan over."

"My first reaction is, that sounds overwhelming," Joanne was honest. "But I'm beginning to understand that my apprehension is just caution. I'm trying to work through my reluctance."

Judith nodded. "Let's start there. Shall we?"

Joanne sat on the black leather couch. "I'm working on Marquel first. But George came to me in a dream again. The same recurring dream. It was different from his visitation." Joanne saw no reason to filter what—to her—was clearly George communicating in spirit.

Judith wasn't certain she heard Joanne correctly. "Wait. Explain his visitation?"

"You'll think I'm crazy. But he came to me. I saw him in a burst of light and he was so sweet and loving. In the dream it was dark and depressing."

"Where were you?"

Joanne put her hand on her forehead. "I was alone in the apartment. I was awake. It wasn't a dream."

"What do you think the visitation was?" Judith began to write.

"I think it was really George. I don't want to call him a ghost. It was his essence. He wanted me to stop being sad and to know he made peace with Zach."

"He made peace with Zach? How do you feel about that?" Judith's tone was even.

"It felt wonderful. He was so handsome, but he was gone quickly when another burst of light came in through the window." Joanne closed her eyes.

She was sure Judith would prescribe something... or wonder if she was taking something.

"Did you see anyone else—in this visitation?"

Joanne shook her head no.

"What do you want to focus on? George's visitation or the dream?"

Joanne sighed. "The visitation. The dream was painful. I woke feeling like I hurt him all over again."

"Do you believe that both manifestations were really George?" Judith asked.

"Yes."

"Do you feel you are receiving mixed messages?" Judith continued.

"No."

"What do you consider a mixed message?" the doctor asked.

Joanne thought. "George said he didn't want me to be sad, but in the dream, he was sad. That's not a mixed message. He could want me to be happy, even though he is sad."

Judith put her pen down. "If George's sadness in the dream makes you sad, but he told you in a manifestation that he wants you to be happy, what do you call that?"

"Manipulation." Joanne seemed to understand.

"Which do you believe?"

"The visit. Because dreams are fears that play out in our unconscious moments." Joanne sat up.

"But some people believe that when a loved one visits in a dream, that is a visitation." Judith studied Joanne's body language.

"Do you believe that, Dr. Wright?" Joanne faced the doctor.

"I'm not sure."

"But George said he made peace with Zach..." Joanne trusted the message.

"Did you want him to make peace?" Judith asked.

Joanne paused. "Of course. But George is not one to give up when he wants something." She choked up. "That's why he was sad in the bar."

"Why?" Judith asked.

"He had to let me go in real life... and the afterlife."

Judith paused. She struggled with her own thoughts of the afterlife. "How do you feel about that?"

"I understand it." Joanne's tone was lighter.

"You do?" Judith was curious.

"Yes, I think I need to return to Florida and say goodbye to the places that were part of my life with Marquel and George." Joanne paused. "I think I'm ready."

Judith made some notes. "I think you are."

CHAPTER THIRTEEN

Marnie loved her shaved head. She took a sample lipstick from the department store counter and drew a red cross on her forehead.

She grabbed a hand mirror off the glass display case and admired herself.

She did a pirouette.

"What do you think? Is it my shade?" Marnie let out a guttural laugh.

The cosmetic clerk gave Marnie a sideways glance.

"Cute," she said, then continued adding makeup to her own face. She couldn't be bothered.

Bart Petty rolled his eyes.

"Great assignment, Rick," he muttered to himself.

Rick Jones tasked Petty to follow the young woman. He was certain Marnie Sikes was up to her old tricks.

Petty snapped a few photos with his pen. He preferred a classic stakeout—distance and a telescopic lens—to this.

His last detail in relation to Joanne Manning was to follow the tabloid journalist Mark Collins the night he lured her for a motorcycle ride.

The ride resulted in what became a shootout on Mt. Lee near the Hollywood sign.

The reporter hadn't realized he was being tailed by a bounty hunter, the Colombian cartel—who brought along a van full of human trafficking victims—Rick Jones and crew, and eventually an LAPD police helicopter.

Collins' goal was to kill Joanne Manning near the Hollywood sign in revenge for his being sent to Bogata by Zach Manning's buddy Lou Bartalow. Instead the reporter lost his own life in the crossfire.

Petty hadn't forgiven himself for getting stuck on the 101 when Mt. Lee was under siege.

Marnie spotted him.

Petty crossed his arms, exposing a small anchor tattoo on his wrist.

He may as well play clothes cop.

She danced over to him. "You're watching me."

Petty was dry. "Store security. Cameras are watching. I'm watching. Passersby... You're pure entertainment."

Marnie hugged him, "That's so adorable."

He pushed her off. "You've crossed the line."

Marnie's eyes got big, mocking him. "What line?"

"This one." He waved his hand at the floor in front of his feet.

"You work for the store or the mall?" Marnie did another pirouette.

He was screwed.

Jones had to take him off the case. They were already too familiar.

"Neither," Petty said.

"What do you do?"

"I follow people like you." He was annoyed.

"Creepy," Marnie liked him.

"Why the mark on your forehead?" He may as well get something to report back.

"I've found Jesus?" She giggled.

"Or Satan?" Petty offered. "Just a hunch."

"Let's go to the food court," Marnie skipped out of the department store.

"I'm not doing that." He cursed himself. "Fucking 101 all over again!"

Jones closed the call with Petty. He couldn't believe it.

Petty blew his cover with Marnie Sikes. The pair had an Orange Julius and bonded over Scooby-Doo mystery references.

Jones couldn't send Dane Blacksmith to follow Sikes, he was the one who caught Marnie breaking and entering at Isabel's on her creepy-crawly mission. Jones had to move Clark Roberts to Marnie's detail and Blacksmith to the foundation. He wasn't about to bring in an unknown.

He looked over at Joanne, she was scrolling through internet travel sites.

Rick unboxed a George Foreman grill.

"I'm dying for a burger. You want one?" He asked Joanne.

"Sure," Joanne clicked through some searches. "I'm going to book a trip."

"Beg your pardon," Rick snapped his gum.

"I've talked to Judith. I need to have closure with Florida," she muttered.

Rick gripped the box he was reading and took a deep breath.

"The state? Not sure this is a good time."

Joanne was becoming sure of the idea, though she was also sure Rick wouldn't go for it right away. "I can go alone. I know the territory."

"Why am I here?" Rick put the box down and walked over to her. He leaned against the wall and crossed his arms. "I'm trying to handle the Marnie situation."

"Is it a situation?" Joanne moved the mouse as she viewed options.

Rick snapped his gum with greater frequency. A dozen responses went through his mind, most of them reactionary and non-helpful. She wasn't going to Florida alone, he damn well knew that much. Then he realized that Marnie didn't know him.

"I'll send Bart Petty to Florida with you." He didn't need to move Clark Roberts from the foundation. Blacksmith would then be free to take on a new client.

He went back to the counter and plugged in the grill.

Joanne rolled her chair back. "Who? Have we met?"

Rick washed his hands up to the wrists in steaming hot water, then shook off the excess moisture and began molding hamburgers with his hands. "You haven't."

He placed one on the grill. It began popping and sizzling. Impressed, he placed another burger on and closed the lid.

"Will I like him?" Joanne asked.

"Probably not, he's got a constipated personality." Rick lifted the lid. "No need to turn. They've thought of everything."

"Smells good," she said.

She took a moment to watch him as he began pulling condiments out of the refrigerator.

"You're really making me hungry," Joanne got up and joined him. "Should I make a salad?"

Rick was back to the grill. He kept opening and closing the grill lid. "How do you want your burger?"

"Well done," Joanne opened the fridge and retrieved a container of potato salad. She didn't really feel like making a tossed salad.

She scooped potato salad onto two plates. She placed mayo, ketchup and mustard on her bun, ketchup and mayo on his.

"I'm rare." Rick muttered. "Almost raw."

He removed his burger and placed it on the dressed bun, bumping up against her unintentionally. "Sorry, boss. And thanks for keeping your hands to yourself."

He was rare all right. Joanne again noticed his well-toned physique, but kept her thoughts about him being *raw* to herself.

Rick grinned at her. He was so amazed by the compact grill.

She blushed. She couldn't remember what they were talking about.

"You're not quite well done." His smile softened.

"I feel well." She got some napkins from a drawer and placed them on the counter next to their plates.

He pressed on the grill and the burger sizzled as liquid grease rolled into a plastic tray. "Bet this could make a mean Cuban."

She nodded, "Florida girls know their Cubans."

Fuck. He didn't like the idea of her being in another state without him.

"Enough about Florida already."

They both paused, the eye contact lasting a little longer than was comfortable.

He turned away, opened the grill and placed her burger on the bun.

"I'm going to book Bart a ticket," she took her plate and moved back to her desk.

Rick unplugged the grill. "Give us a few options. I've got to discuss this with the guys. Too many troop movements."

Rick picked up his plate and moved to the dinette, watching her back.

"I've never understood how a troop could be one person. Sounds like it should be a group." Joanne took a bite of her sandwich. "Hmm."

"You like it?" He was pleased. He began to eat his. "You have to get the right cuts of beef and add seasoning."

"My George was like you. A really great grillsman," Joanne surprised herself. She wasn't consciously thinking of George.

She put her burger down and picked up her plate, joining Rick at the small kitchen table.

"To what do I owe the pleasure?" Rick worked on his potato salad.

"Thank you," Joanne watched him eat. "I am trying to become more independent, or less dependent. I still don't feel like a public figure. I just feel like Joanne, the Florida nobody. And I don't mean that like I'm nobody, but I was just George and Marquel's somebody. That's the way I feel."

He smiled. "Tell me about your daughter."

Joanne's eyes watered. "She was bright, inquisitive, stubborn, and a beautiful soul. She loved to pick wildflowers for me and she once got a bee sting in the process. Nearly broke my heart, she cried so hard."

"Do you have other pictures of her?" Rick asked.

"They're at our... George's house. I took just the one that I have on the desk. I couldn't handle much more when I left." She dabbed her tears with her napkin.

Rick finished chewing and pushed his plate aside. "Let's talk about this. Can you get into the house?"

Joanne nodded. "I know how to get in, but once I married Zach I lost any claim. I haven't tried to do anything—Wait, how do you know I'm going to the house?"

I know you, he wanted to say, but instead said, "You don't need closure with a state, you need closure with your past."

"Then you're okay with the idea."

He shrugged. "The idea is great. Ideas just have a way of morphing into something else when they become reality."

She pushed her potato salad around with her fork. "I suppose that's true."

"So the house just got locked up... George had no next of kin?"

Joanne sighed. "He has a sister. Shit, you're right. She could have sold the place. I've totally forgotten about her. She didn't visit us but a couple of times when we were married."

"Did George get along with her?" Rick realized they'd not discussed George much. In fact, his name had only begun popping up recently.

"Yes. They seemed to think they were normal. Of course, who am I to talk? I didn't have any family to visit. My aunt passed by the time we got married. But if I had a brother or sister, I think I'd want to spend more time with them."

Rick nodded in agreement. "Every family is different. My brothers and parents are in Alaska. They don't travel much. We drop a card or email. A random call. We seem to know when someone is in need and we step up."

"I never thought of myself as an orphan." Joanne got up and took their plates.

"So your plan is to get into the house? Assuming it's as it was," he was back to business.

"I would." Joanne said.

"Okay, I'll see that you're covered." He stood and went to clean the grill, making a mental note to brief Petty himself. He would emphasize professionalism, and strongly suggest his colleague put his own life on the line to protect Joanne's. Which was par for the course, but if Petty was going to stand-in for Rick he'd better be ready to leave it all on the field.

She wished Rick were going. She remembered well how he had carried her away from that horrid scene—the night the hill above the Hollywood sign became a bloody crime scene. His strength was etched in her memory. She could still feel him holding her.

Joanne stopped him. "I can't have everyone cleaning up after me."

"I believe I made this mess."

"Then I should clean," Joanne shooed him out.

"Thank you for joining me for dinner." He winked. "I'll talk to Bart."

That wink. She was glad he was leaving the kitchen.

It might be good to be away from him for a few days. She could focus on the spiritual work she needed to do... then maybe she would be ready to begin a new chapter in her life.

CHAPTER FOURTEEN

Carmen, Isabel's housekeeper, paced the kitchen waiting for her boss.

She'd been the Manning's maid since Jackie was in elementary school. She loved the family, had been with Isabel through her divorce from Zach and later—when the media descended on her—once Zach began treating Marquel.

From a professional perspective, Carmen was now the Herlbert maid, as her friends called her.

Employers were given last name recognition. "Are the Tylers going to Cabo?" "Did the Branson house get damaged in the mudslide?" "What happened to the Stewart boy?"

Her friends were prone to taking sides when employers divorced. The spouse or partner who kept the house wasn't always the favored one.

Carmen remained neutral, she didn't fault Zach for marrying the actress, nor Isabel for despising Zach and Joanne. She understood a woman's scorn, and a child's sympathy for her stepmother.

Carmen didn't know Joanne. Had never met the woman. Which made today's discussion difficult.

Isabel called out, startling Carmen's train of thought. "I'll be there in a moment, Carmen."

Carmen began to talk to herself in Spanish and made a sign of the cross.

Rehearsing made the information easier to relate.

Isabel came into the kitchen with a clean face. No makeup. She was in a one piece white swimsuit and sandals.

She tucked her hair into a white swim cap as she studied Carmen. "Lyle will be home in a few hours, I need to get to my workout. What is it?"

"Meez Isabel, I need to talk to you," Carmen was especially nervous. She knew Isabel was short on patience... and attention span.

"Get on with it," Isabel hadn't seen Carmen this flustered before.

Isabel sat at the kitchen table and motioned for Carmen to do the same.

Carmen rubbed her lips together, then ran her hands over her apron. She sat across from her boss.

Isabel slapped the table. "Spit it out."

Carmen jumped. "I'm afraid."

"Of what?"

The maid teared up.

Isabel was glued to the maid's expression. "God knows we've been through enough. You should be able to tell me anything..." as long as it's relevant, she thought to herself.

Carmen made the sign of the cross again.

"What?!" Isabel couldn't imagine.

"I'm afraid for Miss Joanne." Carmen laced her fingers together like she was in prayer.

Isabel scoffed. "What in God's name has she done now?"

Carmen paused. "This is serious, Meez Isabel."

"It always is. Isn't it?" Isabel wasn't surprised by anything related to Joanne.

"Very serious," Carmen tried not to cry.

"I believe you, Carmen. She's always stirring up trouble." Isabel grabbed a coffee mug off the mug tree in the middle of the table and handed it to Carmen. "Would you mind? I have a feeling this is going to take a while."

Carmen moved quickly. She got up and grabbed the coffee out of the cabinet. She counted scoops into the filter and ran water into the bin.

"Can you talk and do that?" Isabel tapped her fingers on the table.

"I'm ..." Carmen dropped the coffee bag and grounds spilled onto the clean counter.

Isabel threw her head back and closed her eyes. She desperately wanted to get to the point and hit the pool.

Carmen cleaned up the mess and let the coffee brew. "My cousin knows someone who knows someone who is in the Mexican mafia. These are very bad people."

"And?" Isabel said.

"These are very bad people." Carmen repeated, "Very bad."

"Your family member in the Mexican mafia... has something to do with Joanne?" Isabel didn't follow.

Carmen kept her head down. "Not MY family," Carmen whispered. "No. Not my family. It is someone my cousin knows."

Isabel balked. "Carmen, every story about a friend who knows someone is hiding who they really know. I won't judge you..."

The coffeemaker bell rang as it stopped brewing.

"No, not my family," Carmen shook her head.

Isabel motioned for Carmen to make her a cup coffee.

Carmen was confused.

"The coffee," Isabel pointed.

"Oh," Carmen began to make her employer's usual, with cream and low fat sweetener. She then turned and placed the cup, napkin and spoon in front of Isabel.

Isabel looked in the cup, stirring the mixture.

Carmen waited. Isabel was never easily satisfied.

Isabel tasted the coffee. "Go on."

Carmen sat. "They want to kill her."

"Your cousins?" Isabel said.

Carmen whispered, "No. The Mexican mafia."

"CARMEN! How do you know this?" Isabel wasn't buying her story.

"I JUST told you! My cousin knows someone who knows someone who is in the Mexican mafia."

Isabel shook her head. "You are confused. Those were Colombians, and their leader is in jail."

"No, Meez Isabel. It is the Mexican mafia. They are seeking revenge," Carmen got up and looked out the kitchen window.

"Why are you doing that? Are you expecting someone?" Isabel was perturbed.

"You believe me?" Carmen wanted an answer.

"No." Isabel said. "I think your cousin's friend's friend is confused." Isabel took another sip. "This needs more sweetener. I have no idea why they're telling you this."

Carmen gave Isabel more sweetener, careful not to spill any.

"Carmen, you remember the incident at the Hollywood sign. The drug lord... and Joanne was in the middle. *Entertainment Tonight* had that whole expose on the siege at Mt. Lee."

Carmen crossed her arms.

"Don't." Isabel scolded, "You look childish."

Carmen began spraying counter tops and wiping them down. She didn't like it when people didn't believe her.

Isabel drank her coffee and watched her maid. She'd known Carmen for years, though the exact number escaped her at the moment. She found the whole thing preposterous. "Why revenge? What has she done?"

Carmen paused. "I don't know. I don't know. I don't know."

Isabel took another sip. "It sounds like you don't know."

Carmen thought a moment. They both laughed, though it was obvious Carmen's laugh had its origin in nerves.

Carmen moved back to the table. "As God is my witness, if I didn't tell you and Miss Joanne died, I would hope God strikes me dead."

"Well we don't want that," Isabel slapped the table again. "I'm not ready to break in a new maid."

Carmen smiled. "Thank you."

Isabel reciprocated. "Do you feel better?"

Carmen nodded.

"So, what am I supposed to do with this information?" Isabel asked.

"Tell the police or Mr. Lyle, they'll know what to do," Carmen was sure.

Isabel shook her head. "You tell the police."

"They won't listen to me." Carmen threw up her hands. "The maids and gardeners in Brentwood know what happened. The ex-wife dies. Poof. The staff know more than the police! No one asks. No one cares. We are nobody unless we are we cleaning your house or pool or toilet ..."

Isabel stopped her. She could see Carmen's point, "I'll tell Lyle."

Carmen made a sign of the cross. "Thank you, Jesus."

"How about thank you, Isabel?"

The maid smiled again, clearly relieved. "Thank you, Meez Isabel."

Revenge? Isabel couldn't imagine.

Gallo confronted Vasquez in the yard.

"A present," he handed Humberto a stack of black and white photos.

Vasquez sorted through them.

It was Joanne moving about her day. Sometimes with a man; in others she looked to be alone.

"We're going to kill her," Gallo's tone was cool. "We'll be sure to send you a little something, to remember her."

Humberto wanted to choke the old man.

Gallo's men outnumbered his.

"What do you want?" Vasquez remained calm.

"Your people out of my territory. There's no room. *Comprenez vous?*" Gallo ripped up the photos.

Vasquez laughed. "No, no, no. Vasquez have the west coast."

"Her days are numbered."

Gallo left Humberto to process the information, walking with his posse.

They communicated amongst themselves in their customary sign language.

CHAPTER FIFTEEN

Josh curled up next to his snoring fiancé and kissed her on the head.

Jackie stirred and moaned.

"Josh," she muttered. She had been sleeping hard enough to leave creases across her face and drool on her pillow.

It was 3am and he was beat, ready to sleep. He thought Jackie was especially adorable when she didn't know he was watching. He could tell she was exhausted.

"It's me," he rubbed her back. "Wait, were you expecting someone else?"

She sat up suddenly.

"I ate too much cake—I think I'm going to throw up," she bolted out of the bed.

Josh watched as she threw open the bathroom door and vomited in the toilet.

"Guess we're not choosing that baker for our wedding cake." He put his head back on the pillow.

"N..." She threw up more.

"Want me to get you some ginger ale?" He'd been working doubles every other day and they barely had time together. Maybe she was coming down with something.

She washed her face and gargled, then stumbled back into bed.

He noticed she seemed puffy. His brows furrowed, "When was your last period, Jackie?"

"Don't… I'm so tired. I just want to sleep." She got under the duvet and wrapped her leg and arm over him.

He kissed her head again and whispered, "We need to move the wedding date up."

She rubbed her eyes. "Is it the hospital? Or that jerk Dr. Cody! Is he going to ruin this?!"

"You're pregnant," he sat up.

Jackie looked at him like she was in a dream. "No, I'm not."

"When was your last period, Jackie?"

She thought. "I'm tired. I don't know."

Josh remembered. Not because he wanted to, but because they had a big fight.

"It's coming any day?" She didn't sound convinced.

"Remember when we fought about whether a tomato was a fruit or vegetable?" He reminded her.

"It is a fruit," she said through her teeth.

"Okay, we're not debating that now," Josh said. "But the last time… you were so pissed off because your period was about to start. That's what *you* said."

Jackie remembered. "Yeah."

"That was two months ago, because I couldn't finish watching the Angels game. You turned off the T.V. and took the remote with you to the donut shop."

She laughed.

"Ha-ha," he mocked. "I can laugh now. Have you had a period since?"

Her eyes got big. "I've had irregular periods before. And televisions work without remotes… believe it or not."

His eyes teared up. "I'm totally okay—if you're okay—with us being pregnant?"

"What?" She didn't want to think about this.

She wanted to be a bride first.

They both yawned and looked at each other.

She touched her stomach. "I thought I was bloating."

"We'll get a pregnancy test in the morning."

He began to cry.

She held him. It touched her that he was so happy.

She wanted to be happy, but she needed to know.

"Let's try to sleep." She kissed him.

"I don't think I can." He pulled her close, "I love you so much."

Joanne and Bart Petty boarded the plane for Gainesville, Florida.

She had not expected to gain Rick's agreement so easily. She was sure he'd come up with more reasons she should hold off traveling.

Petty drank a diet soda and kept his eye on the incoming passengers.

"Have you ever been to Florida?" Joanne asked.

Petty kept watch as he talked, "Not to Gainesville. Miami yes."

Joanne took a deep breath. She saw a younger man very similar to George come through first class and pass them.

Rick insisted they travel first class, though she'd rather not.

"You look like you've seen a ghost," Petty observed. "Do you know that man? Is there something I should be aware of?"

"No." Joanne relaxed. "He looks a lot like my first husband." She couldn't believe she said *first*. How is it that she had already had two husbands?

"Roger that. The one who lived in Gainesville," Petty nodded.

His senses were on overload. Jones had made it abundantly clear that he shadow Joanne at all times, as well as remain aware of all possible threats—and maybe even impossible threats. As a result he had done all but check the wings of the plane for gremlins.

"Near Gainesville," she corrected. "You'll see."

She turned to look for the man who resembled George, but the privacy curtain in first class was closed.

CHAPTER SIXTEEN

DEA agent Barry Liebold was tasked with finding a way to secure Humberto Vasquez's cooperation.

The Mexican mafia was growing territory faster than the agency could monitor. They needed the Vasquez cartel to wipe out Mexican mafia leaders and slow Gallo's expansion.

In return, the DEA would provide Humberto safe passage back to Colombia—if he agreed to stay out of the U.S.

But how?

Liebold met with Jeremiah Wakes at the prison. The agency discovered members of Vasquez's crew were in and out of the guard's homestead with regularity. As well, Wakes had recently acquired 100 acres adjacent.

"We need your help," Liebold pushed a photo in front of Wakes. "This your property?"

Wakes glanced, pushed the paper back. "It is."

"What are your plans?" The seasoned DEA man asked. The agency had flown over the undeveloped property. It showed no signs of farming or meth labs.

"To be a poppy farmer," Wakes laughed. "That what you want to hear?"

Liebold smiled back. He didn't like a smart ass.

Wakes shook his head. "I've got heads to bust."

"About that," Liebold was direct, "there'll come a time when your number's up. The liberals will send in human rights attorneys and you'll be living with the animals as one. The cameras catch everything."

Wakes stared. Said nothing.

Liebold showed him a diagram. "We're thinking we lure Gallo's people out to an area where—possibly—the Vasquez cartel might ambush them... Your acreage could prove to be an ideal spot. It's quiet, remote."

"And I'm the animal?" Wakes chuckled, "Go ahead. Might have my name on it but I didn't ask for it. Happy to see all these fuckers go up in a blaze of gunfire."

"We need Gallo to buy in. Otherwise, they'll assume it's a bust and nobody makes a move."

"Provided they show up." Wakes eyed Liebold. *Dumb fucker,* he thought.

"That's where you come in," Liebold gave Wakes a nod.

"Me?" Wakes didn't follow.

"We've got hours of tape. The surveillance footage shows Gallo signing to his guys that he wants to get even with Humberto Vasquez." Liebold got up and paced, digging his hands in his pockets.

"You watched for hours? They say that in passing," Wakes laughed and put his feet up on the table. He placed his hands behind his head, "I'm all ears."

The agent continued, "It's no secret Humberto is obsessed with the actress Marquel, AKA civilian Joanne Manning. Gallo's people are watching her closely."

Wakes' brows arched. "The Mexicans are watching her?"

Liebold nodded.

"Finally, something I've not heard." Wakes was still unimpressed with the DEA agent.

"We want Joanne Manning to go with the Mexicans to your property, luring Vasquez to save her. Then we get her out and eliminate the Mexican threat," Liebold said.

"You just said you wanted to lure Mexicans a minute ago. But now you want a civilian decoy to bring them together, so you can take out the Mexicans and let Vasquez go home?" Wakes asked. He also had his doubts about the DEA's ability to protect a civilian in such an operation, but he kept his opinion to himself.

"The Colombians have a smaller footprint in the U.S. We need a big shakeup before the next election. The president needs this. We must lessen the Gallo stronghold," Liebold sat and looked Wakes in the eye. "Can we count on you?"

Wakes dropped his feet to the floor. "Me?"

Liebold nodded. "Yes, help us get Vasquez on board."

Wakes was frank. "No."

"What if we convince Joanne Manning to help us?" The agent was serious.

"And you think I'm a prick?" Wakes pointed to himself. "You'd rather use a traumatized woman to lure two rival gangs to kill each other?"

"We're not going to let anything happen to her," Liebold was confident.

Wakes shook his head. "What the fuck is wrong with this country?"

"It's complicated." Liebold crossed his arms.

"No," Wakes said. "It's not. But shit like this is... I take my rage out on guys who hurt innocent people, but I wouldn't ask an innocent woman to be bait for a plan that has a fifty percent—at best—chance of working."

"Do you have a better idea?" Liebold asked.

"Kill the Mexicans yourself. Hell, wipe out the Colombians, too." Wakes threw his hands in the air, "This one's on you."

"And then a bigger threat emerges from inside of either cartel... making matters worse," Liebold countered. "Been there, done that. We need to let *them* level the playing field. Besides, we have good relations with the Colombians."

"Oh really, what are the Colombians doing for you?"

"Sharing information. In return, we let them enter the country."

Wakes laughed. "And once they're in the country you arrest them, so I can crack their heads?"

"That *is* one way they grow their trade inside the prison."

Wakes hadn't realized the bastards wanted in. He felt his blood pressure shoot up.

"You can take the property. Seize it," Wakes got up to leave. Liebold was disappointed.

"We know Vasquez is taking care of you and your family. We know everything," Liebold said.

"*They* involved my family, I didn't. I have way more to lose than a fucking election!" Wakes spat.

"Then help us," Liebold pleaded.

"They'll find out your plan."

"How?" Liebold asked.

"I'll tell him." Wakes punched the wall as he exited.

Joanne and Petty walked the perimeter of the property, mosquitoes buzzing around them.

Joanne slapped her arm. "I forgot how bad they are," she fanned her face with one hand, keeping the other in front of her to catch spider webs before they covered the two of them.

Petty watched the ground for snakes, cursing the assignment silently.

He remembered Jones breaking the good news/bad news when he gave the order: "The good news is you're accompanying a beautiful Hollywood icon to the sunshine state. Bad news? Fuck it up and I'll kill you."

If he had wondered if Rick had a personal involvement with Joanne Manning, the question was answered then and there. Maybe Rick hadn't realized it himself yet, and if Bart had pressed the issue Jones would've reminded him how he fucked up the Sikes surveillance—Bart kept his mouth shut.

"You lived out here?" Petty was surprised.

She smiled. "You don't know me."

"I'm beginning to," Petty slapped his face, pulling a bloody mosquito corpse off and flicking it aside.

The thigh high grass had signs posted: "No Trespassing."

"I can hunt, fish… even build a fire."

"You'd have to." He looked around, "To live off the grid."

"I've always had power," she made her way to the porch.

She really missed George and Marquel at this moment. She desperately hoped the photos were still in the house.

Petty climbed onto the porch, looking in the windows on either side of the front door.

It was dusk. The weather was humid, but the temperature was dropping slightly.

She found the bucket that she and George kept hidden. It was covered in cobwebs.

"Careful," Petty cautioned. "Might be a brown recluse in there."

"If a spider is going to take me out now, then it was meant to be." She didn't hesitate and grabbed for the key at the bottom. She then hung the bucket on a rusted hook.

Her eyes teared up. She realized some things didn't change.

She took a deep breath.

"Are you okay?" He asked.

"Not really," she moved to the door, unlocking the knob first, then the deadbolt.

Petty drew his sidearm and entered ahead of her, "Wait here."

She ignored his command and followed him in, hoping he didn't disturb anything as he went from room, checking corners and behind doors.

It was hot inside. She began opening windows to release the heat.

Everything was left intact, to her memory. Even the final letter she had written to George was still on the table. It was like a stab in the heart.

"You're clear," Petty took his place by the screen door.

He hoped to hell it would be a short visit, he wasn't the type to provide emotional support. He slapped his face again. *Fucking mosquitoes.*

Her rifle was still on the wall. She sighed.

George's was the instrument that killed him. It was in police custody.

The sheriff reported that George had the barrel pointed toward his abdomen and had struck the butt of the rifle against a tree. The coroner indicated he likely would have survived the wound to his side, as no vital organs were struck. It was the blow to his head that killed him. George stumbled backward after the bullet made impact, hitting his head against a stump.

Joanne moved to the back of the house, going into Marquel's room.

She took in her surroundings—the changing table with stuffed animals lining the shelves, the open closet. All of little Marquel's clothes were still hanging, faded and dusty in a rainbow of cottons, knits and taffeta. Her baby doll Cara was on the floor.

Joanne knelt by the small toddler bed with the Strawberry Shortcake comforter and everything came flooding back.

A burst of light from the setting sun shone through a crack in the curtains.

"Joanne?" She heard a familiar voice.

She turned. There was no one there. Then she heard a giggle.

She turned back to the light between the curtains.

She stood and opened the window. A gentle breeze moved the cotton fabric.

"Joanne it's me." The voice again.

"George?" She whispered.

Then she saw him.

He looked like he did the day they married. His reassuring grin always told her he was up to something.

Bart Petty called out, "You okay?"

"Yes," Joanne responded quickly, loud enough for Petty to keep his post.

She didn't need anyone to intrude on this moment.

George stayed where he was. A spirit or a hologram, she wasn't certain.

"Roger that," Petty shouted back.

She sat on the child's bed and asked George, "Why?"

"I'm waiting for someone to take care of you."

He knelt beside her. Tears spilled from her eyes.

She adored his straight nose and perfect mouth. His short sandy hair was hidden under a John Deere ball cap. He was an all-American in faded denim. Never looked better.

"We don't have to say goodbye," George reassured her. "Remember the time you and Marquel planted those sunflower seeds? They never grew—that's what you thought. Look out the window."

She pulled the curtains back and saw the towering sunflowers. Hundreds of them.

"Oh George." She cried, "I never noticed them when I came home with you."

"You have to open your heart and allow yourself to see beauty again." He spoke softly, "You have so much more life to live. You're making a difference in so many people's lives."

Just then Petty walked in and saw her sobbing.

George left through the light between the curtains.

Petty returned to the front of the house, reassured she was safe and alone in the room. He had no business trying to understand what she was going through. *Just do the job.*

Joanne got up and walked slowly to the bedroom she shared with George.

She sat on double bed, running her hand over the bedspread. The white chenille was dry rotting and the bed seemed so much smaller than she remembered. The ten by ten foot room had an oak chest of drawers and a dresser squeezed in opposite the bed. Several family photos hung above the chest.

It was getting dark.

With the power off, she needed to close everything and head out.

She met Petty by the screen door, "I want to come back in the morning."

He gave her a quick nod, then scanned the exterior again.

"Or we could stay overnight if you're adventurous," she said. "I could cook something on the cast iron stove. We only used it in the winter. We used the electric stove for every day."

Petty slapped a mosquito that got in, "No thanks. Sounds like pure hell cooking inside this sauna. We can go to a truckstop."

Joanne sat down at the table.

"George worked at a truckstop." She picked up his letter and stared at it.

"Wait," Petty held a hand up. Jones had filled him in on the few details he had about Joanne's former home, but something didn't make sense. "Back up. Your husband worked at a truckstop, and yet no one saw you on Suburban Life? No one told him?"

"Most locals still use rabbit ears to get a television signal, and that doesn't always work." She placed the letter back on table. "Some can't even tell you who the governor is. We only got videos after the hardware store started selling VHS players. And George never cared about television. He liked to sit outside. Listen to the crickets and the rain. He read Field and Stream and his mechanic magazines. He was teaching Marquel about bugs, reptiles, flowers and deer."

Petty wasn't convinced. "No. Hold the phone. Everyone had to know about the horrible accident that killed your daughter—her name had to be circulating in local gossip. Plus, you disappeared. And they saw George alone. Something doesn't add up."

"Bart, it's different here." She pushed her hair back behind her ears, wishing she had put it up before they came out here. Florida heat could all but crawl inside someone and take over. "People didn't talk to us about it. They didn't want to say anything that might add to our pain."

"Then why didn't anyone look for you? If they cared so much?"

"Because George didn't tell them I was gone." She hadn't really thought about it. It hurt to realize how George's pride and her shame pushed her to the extreme.

Petty noted a change, she was pissed at George. He was sorry he brought it up.

"He was angry at me and hurt. He blamed me for Marquel's death and he really didn't care at first. I was dead to him. He wasn't going to tell anyone until he absolutely had to."

Beads of perspiration burst from Petty's pores, soaking his head and collar.

Joanne's face grew a healthy shade of red.

"Thanks for clearing that up," Petty said finally. "I'm cooking internally, so... when you're ready."

"I'll close the windows." Joanne got up, leaving the letter on the table.

She went back and grabbed a few pictures off the bedroom wall, then returned to her daughter's room to close the window.

She looked out the curtain again. The sunflowers were gone.

She knew George brought her the flowers.

She closed the window, grabbed Cara and hugged her tightly. She could almost feel her daughter hugging her back.

Marnie showed up at COR in a frilly peasant top and shorts. She thought she'd surprise Humberto and give him an update on her progress with Joanne—not that there was any. She just wanted to see him. Surprise him with her new look.

Her hair had grown some. It looked like soft peach fuzz.

She still wore bold eyeliner. Her complexion glowed, thanks to a creamy foundation and soft pink blush she was trying. Her lips pale pink.

She sat in the waiting area among the other inmates' friends and family.

She brought a magazine but was too distracted to read. She flipped the pages until her name was called. She couldn't figure out where it was coming from.

It was one of the prison guards, who verified she was alone.

As such, he had been told to inform her that Humberto refused to see her.

Fuck! Now she had to drive back.

She threw the magazine in the trash.

Why was Joanne so fucking special?

She had to move on a plan.

As she was about to leave, a man with a crew cut stopped her.

He had overheard she was there for Vasquez, would she answer a few questions?

Marnie could tell this guy was a cop or a lawyer. He suggested they get coffee somewhere and talk, which she could only assume might have negative repercussions for Humberto.

Like he gave a shit.

"Sure," Marnie said. "I'll let you buy me a burger. I'm starving."

He wrote directions to a small diner about 15 minutes down the road. He had to gather up a few things, then he'd meet her there.

Which suited Marnie. She didn't want to be seen leaving with the guy, just in case word got back to Humberto.

Greta and Ken met in his office. They were both struggling.

His only bankable property had been Marquel. He was living off his cut of Joanne's residuals, which were limited, given the show never hit season three. But it played well in syndication on obscure cable channels and in overseas markets—and *Suburban Life* was now a VHS title, moving into DVD distribution. The new revenue stream was promising.

Greta stared at Ken's bar in the corner of the office.

"What's up, doll?" Ken sat behind his desk.

She turned to meet his question. She loved being around him.

Ken crossed his right leg, then decided to change position and sit on his left leg, keeping his right foot on the floor.

Greta smiled at him. "I was thinking we should team up."

Ken switched to both feet on the floor. "My foot's numb. Should I get my circulation checked?"

She shook her head.

"Team up?" He echoed and drummed on his desk top. "Avery-Goldberg... sounds like trial attorneys. I like it! I'll be Corbin Bersen and you'll be Susan Dey. I loved *L.A. Law*."

"Me too," Greta agreed.

Ken opened his desk drawer and took a pen out. He began to twirl it through his fingers.

Greta pushed a post-it caddy in front of him. "Write it down?"

Ken's mouth dropped in excitement. "We should!"

He wrote: Entertainment Practice. Avery-Goldberg. Office hours...

"What will our office hours be?"

Greta was relieved he liked the idea. She'd been running low on ideas for awhile.

"Wednesday through Friday, eleven to four."

Ken wrote it down, raising an eyebrow. "What will we do on Monday and Tuesday?"

"Lunch," Greta's smile grew.

"Perfect!" Ken wrote LUNCH and peeled the post-it off the cube. He handed it to Greta, "That will be $200. My hourly."

"Bill me," Greta handed it back.

"That will incur further handling," he scratched over the whole thing and wrote $250. "That's thirty days net, sister!"

She saluted him. "Net."

Ken scratched his head and whispered, "I can't keep net and gross straight."

"We'll have accountants for that," she whispered back.

Ken nodded, not certain if they were having fun or really talking business.

There was a long pause. Greta got up.

"Thanks, Ken."

She knew this would never work. Or rather, they'd never get around to doing any work.

"Where are you going?" Ken followed her to the door.

She kissed him on the cheek. "You always make me feel wonderful."

"Get back in here." He was sincere, "What's this really about?"

Greta teared up. "I'm afraid."

"Afraid of what?"

She dropped her head on his shoulder. "That I'll never find a decent film. That I'm washed up."

Ken squeezed her. "What's today?"

"Tuesday," Greta sniffled.

Ken pulled back and looked her in the eye, "Avery-Goldberg Entertainment Practitioners don't waste time in the office on Tuesdays. We lunch!"

She dabbed her eyes with the tips of her fingers. "But really, Ken. We can't do this. We'd never get any work done."

Ken nodded his head, "We should totally do this! You are a very successful producer. I'm a mouthpiece. I can drum up business that I have no business managing."

"Really?" She gave him the most doe-eyed expression.

He couldn't hurt Bambi.

"What do we have to lose?"

Agent Liebold slid into the booth opposite Marnie and placed his business card in front of her.

"You're late." She read the card, "Barry. Lie. Bold. I was going to eat and skip out on the check if you didn't show."

The waitress interrupted, she had already served Marnie several glasses of water, "Are you ready to order?"

"Hell yeah," Marnie handed her the menu. "Patty melt, rare. Fries, large chocolate shake and maybe pie later."

Agent Liebold faked a smile, "Chef salad with Italian dressing and a coffee. Black."

Marnie wanted whatever the government was buying. "I'll take a tank of gas, too."

"We'll see."

Marnie moved the ketchup and salt and pepper to the middle of the table, lining them up like little soldiers between them. "So, DEA, huh? You want to talk about the cartel?"

She didn't know shit about the cartel, but that fact could wait until after Liebold paid the check.

"Actually, we understand you know Joanne Manning..."

He had barely finished speaking the name when Marnie shouted loud enough for the cooks to hear, "Fuck Joanne Manning! Why is everyone so fucking enamored with her?!"

Liebold held up both hands. "Aren't you friends with her stepdaughter?"

Marnie shrugged. "Haven't talked to her in forever... is this about Joanne or Jackie?"

"It's about you," the agent could tell that's what she wanted to hear.

Marnie bounced in her seat and smiled big.

The waitress placed a large chocolate shake with whipped cream and a cherry in front of Marnie, then poured a coffee for Liebold.

"Oh my god that looks good," Marnie took a big slurp through the straw. "I'm going to orgasm."

Liebold watched her pull the straw out halfway and suck on the whipped cream. She grabbed the cherry and held it over her mouth by the stem, then bit it in half and placed the remains back on top of the whipped cream.

The kid was quite the showgirl, he had to wonder if he could work her. Stable and low-key were not the terms that came to mind as he observed her.

The waitress returned shortly with their meals.

"Thank you!" Marnie was so happy. She shook the ketchup bottle and uncapped it, but the thick liquid didn't move. She took her knife and stabbed around inside the upside down bottle until it gushed enough ketchup to cover the fries.

Liebold cut his salad and tossed the Italian dressing in. He took a bite, chewing while Marnie was slurping her shake in between big bites of her patty melt.

"I'm just going to talk," he took a sip of coffee, "and you fill me in."

Marnie nodded.

"I think you could help us, since you're friends with Humberto Vasquez."

"He proposed, you know... Are you working with him?" Marnie held a fry and licked at the ketchup. "Are you on the take?"

Liebold smiled. "No."

"With a name like Lie. Bold?"

"Funny," he didn't laugh.

"What about Joanne?" Marnie ate the other half of her cherry.

"Why eat a small cherry in two bites?" He took a bite of salad, curious as to her answer.

Instead Marnie slurped her milkshake and watched him eat. She held up one finger until the shake was gone, then she answered. "Someone told me that love is an ice cream sundae and sex is the cherry on top. I want sex to last, you know."

He hadn't heard that one before. She picked up the burger and ate another bite.

He changed the subject. "You said Humberto proposed. Did you accept?"

"Duh. Yeah," Marnie beamed.

"What happens if he never gets out?"

Marnie was way ahead of him, "I'm going to get a marriage license when we set the date. We'll marry and I'll visit him regularly. If he wants me to meet his family in Colombia, I'll go..."

Liebold was not surprised by Marnie's naivete, nor her arrest at Isabel Manning's. "Are you involved in his organization?"

"Hmm." She wanted to be, "Sadly, no."

She made a pouty face, then grabbed her fork and took a bite of his salad.

"Yuck," she spit it on her plate.

"Would you live in Colombia with him, if he ever gets out?" Liebold asked.

Marnie played with the last French fry and leftover ketchup.

Liebold pushed the unfinished salad away and motioned to the waitress to bring him more coffee.

The waitress looked at Marnie's plate and then to Liebold as she filled his cup.

Liebold glanced over and noticed the word PIG spelled out in ketchup.

"You can take our plates. I'm finished," he told the waitress.

When she had walked away he turned back to Marnie. "Favorite Manson quote?"

Marnie giggled, "Doodling."

He knew she was messing with him. Two could play that game, "Have you visited Charlie Manson? He's at Corcoran, too." Liebold knew she hadn't, Manson's visitors were well documented, but he wondered about her capacity for honesty. Or recognizing reality, for that matter.

"No. He's getting old, really starting to lose it. Sad," she grabbed the dessert menu. "Humberto is way more powerful."

He nodded, "Let's get back to Joanne Manning. Are you aware of the Vasquez family... *obsession* with the actress' persona Marquel?"

Marnie rolled her eyes. "It's so embarrassing."

"She lacks your youth. So, she's no threat to your future plans with Vasquez, right?"

Marnie thought about it.

Liebold posed the question, "What do you think Vasquez would do, if he had a chance to meet her again?"

"Kidnap her and take her to Colombia," Marnie blurted without hesitation.

"If he met her at the prison?" Liebold clarified.

"I wish I knew," Marnie was curt.

The waitress placed the check on the table.

Marnie handed it back to her. "I want apple pie. A la mode."

Liebold nodded. "Make it two."

The waitress left.

"You said this is all about *me*, and how is that?" Marnie wasn't believing him.

"Can you keep this to yourself?" The agent asked, leaning toward her. He didn't wait for her answer, "We might make a deal with Vasquez. If we do, then you might get a chance to live with your groom in Colombia."

The waitress refilled the agent's coffee cup, "Pie's coming."

Marnie beamed. "Yes! Wait. What's Joanne got to do with this?"

"We need a carrot... to get Vasquez' cooperation. But you'll be waiting for him."

Marnie reached for one of the pie plates the waitress brought to their table.

"So you trick him? Then he gets pissed at me."

"But you'll turn the charm on, win him over," Liebold gave her a nod.

Marnie wasn't convinced. She took a bite of pie.

"He's been in COR long enough to... well, let's just say it'll probably take you less than one night to convince him he belongs with you."

He could see her eyes light up at the thought. She bounced on her seat.

"So how are you getting Joanne involved?" Marnie talked with her mouth full.

The agent took a bite of his pie. "What would you suggest?"

This could be her chance. She continued to eat and think.

The agent watched her.

"How about *you* find a way to get Joanne there. Let him think I made the arrangement." *Marnie wins all,* she thought. "Humberto believes I am trustworthy and will fall head over heels in love with me."

"Fall?" The agent laughed and ate another bite of pie. "He proposed to *you,* did he not?"

Marnie's excitement grew. She knew there was a way she could make this work for her, but there had to be more to the agent's proposition.

"Why do you need me?" She was not sure what the DEA was really up to. "This is all pretty fucked up. I mean, Humberto wants to see her. You want him to see her... And somehow I'm in the middle?"

"Who else would be the perfect liaison?" Liebold waved a spoonful of vanilla ice cream. "You have an existing relationship with both Vasquez and Manning."

"Liaison," she muttered.

She finished her pie.

"So you'll help us?"

She grinned. "Hell yeah."

Joanne and Petty loaded the rented SUV with photos and a few family mementos. She also took the Strawberry Shortcake comforter and the chenille bedspread. She wasn't certain what she'd do with the chenille, but it could be repurposed.

She'd also get new bed linens soon. She realized she was still sleeping on the set she and Zach shared. Time to make a change. She didn't want to pine over George or Zach.

They drove to the Old Grove Cemetery in Gulf Hammock where little Marquel was buried. She couldn't bring herself back to the graveside after her service. She couldn't, wouldn't let herself believe her daughter was gone, let alone under the dirt.

The shell drive crunched as they entered the small stretch of civil war era headstones. Most families in the area had newer plots in the north section.

Her eyes came upon the small granite cross and beside it a slightly larger granite cross. Marquel Jennings and George Jennings and the dates of their birth and death. Daughter and father rested side by side.

She gasped as she saw the cross beside George bore her name and birth date.

"Oh my God!" Joanne felt sick.

Petty parked the vehicle and followed her to the headstones.

"George must have..." she choked on the words, pointing instead.

Now he understood. George's headstone appeared to have a plate added where the death date appeared. The headstone for Joanne was missing a death date.

"You didn't know?" asked Petty.

Joanne threw her head back, closing her eyes. "I wouldn't go to the grave after Marquel died. He must have bought them shortly after she passed."

Petty nodded. "Not being disrespectful, but what bothers you about this?"

She turned to face him, noticed his eyes watering. "Did you lose someone?"

"My high school sweetheart died in a boating accident our senior year. I always thought I would be buried next to her if I never married." Petty began to choke up.

Joanne put a hand on his shoulder. She hoped it reassured him, but it helped her to remember others had their losses too. Neither of them had to be alone in their pain.

He didn't like the silence that had enveloped the cemetery, so he went on just to break it. "I bought a plot next to her when I was 21, with my savings."

Joanne placed her hand over mouth.

"Susie, my girlfriend, came to me in dreams for a long time after she died. Not so much anymore," he trailed off. Something about graveyards, he pressed his thumb and forefinger against the bridge of his nose.

Joanne couldn't bring herself to tell him about George's visits.

He sniffed, "I'll get your flowers."

Joanne had bought potted mums in yellow and white. She wanted to plant them during the hot and rainy season, in hopes they would come back each year.

Petty came back with the flower pot under one arm and a bag of potting soil on his shoulder. She took the potted mums and sat them down as he laid the bag on the ground and returned to the car.

Joanne fell into step with Petty. "I'll get the water jugs. Did we bring the hand spade?"

"All on the back seat," he replied.

When they were done, they spread extra potting soil on the sandy spots where grass wasn't growing. She had left her grave bare.

Then an idea struck her.

She went back to the car and grabbed the chenille bedspread. She draped it over her cross to shroud it, tying two corners together on the back side.

"It's not going to last," Petty stated the obvious.

She took out a small camera and took pictures of the three graves. Then she bent down to kiss Marquel's and George's crosses.

"A part of me died when Marquel died, and again when I was shot. A child is your flesh. A portion of you. I'm at peace that George is with her."

Joanne gathered the empty soil bags and water jugs and made her way to the car, feeling her spirits lift just a bit.

Petty followed, closing the hatch on the SUV before climbing back into the driver's seat. Joanne joined him on the passenger side, buckling her seatbelt.

"Thank you for sharing your story about Susie. It helped me," Joanne was sincere.

Petty nodded.

"I want to show you the old theater," she changed the subject.

She had worked there briefly after she left George. She had once suppressed these memories. It wasn't until Judith introduced hypnotherapy that she began to recall how she got to California.

In her first session of hypnosis she saw her bare feet in the woods. They were dirty and bleeding. She was looking down. Her hair cascading like a waterfall. She had searched for her daughter in the swamp adjacent to the hunt club. The sessions opened her mind to a series of scenes that converged over time.

"Turn here." Joanne directed Petty to a stretch of two lane highway near Otter Creek, letting her window down. Warm air blew her hair around as strands and clumps covered her face. She let it fly as she kept watch for deer and cattle in the miles of pasture before them.

Petty observed her. She was a natural beauty. Her hair the color of ripe corn silk.

He left his window up. Giving her the chance to have the comfort of air conditioning while experiencing the scents of the countryside.

"Is it far?" Petty asked.

"About 35 minutes," Joanne spoke over the sound of the tires.

"How did you end up that far away?" Petty asked.

"Walked." Joanne leaned back into her seat, "I didn't realize that I was homeless, until the couple who owned the theater took me in."

"How long were you out wandering?" He couldn't imagine it being long in the swampy terrain. "You must have been eaten up by mosquitoes."

"That's a blur. I was very sunburned. It's amazing how people look away." She closed her window, "You know."

He knew. He could see himself not making eye contact with her—hoping someone else would. "I think I do."

She touched his arm. "People don't know how to deal with painful situations. That's partially why I started the foundation—to make a difference for women who have been forgotten."

Petty nodded.

After a minute or so riding in silence, she opened her window again, crossed her arms and leaned out. She let the sound of rushing wind beat in her ears and toss her hair.

Petty turned on the radio.

It was a straight two lane highway that gave them both a chance to unwind.

"Will the theater owners be in?" Petty hadn't expected to see miles and miles of roadway with only an occasional pickup truck or semi passing through. The lack of traffic relaxed him.

She turned to him and spoke loudly. "I haven't been in touch."

He nodded.

She looked ahead. "Turn left at the light."

The intersection had a flashing red light and a cluster of small crosses at one corner of the intersection.

"Looks like a family," she pointed to the crosses.

"Maybe two," Petty acknowledged. "Fatal for all parties."

"I hope no one survived." She kept an eye on the mock gravesite as they turned.

"I hear you." Petty eyed the crosses in the rearview mirror.

They came into Newberry and a stretch of shops a mile in length. It was a cluster of essentials. An ammo shop, a thrift store, a diner, grocer, appliance shop, gas station. Army surplus, lawyer, post office and church.

Petty stopped at the gas station. "How much further?"

"Five or ten minutes." Joanne stayed in the car.

He opened his door and stepped out.

She watched him pump gas.

He was a good man. Much different than Rick described.

Once they were back on the road they saw random clusters of old cracker homes with raised porches, peeling paint and jalousie windows. The closer they got to High Springs, the nicer the redeveloped historic properties appeared.

She recognized a section of shotgun homes near the railroad track.

"I followed the track," she remembered. "It was a beautiful moonlit night. The deer who grazed nearby... They watched me. We all lived out under the stars."

Petty dropped his speed through the small downtown. "Where to?"

"Turn here, then next right." She grew excited.

They stopped in front of a red brick building whose old marquee was damaged. KEEP AWAY signs were posted in several conspicuous places.

The Day Dream Theater was boarded up. The remaining letters in the marquee read:

Tha _ks for _ _ _ Memorie_.

"Seems poetic," Petty said. "Thanks for the Memories."

Joanne sighed, "Thanks for *memory*." She got out of the SUV.

Petty parked the vehicle and joined her. "What's next."

She turned to face him.

"This chapter is closed."

CHAPTER SEVENTEEN

Isabel waited outside the restaurant. She'd arrived early, wanting to see if any who's who were in the immediate area.

Sam Kindred waved from a table in front of the eatery, nestled by the garden.

Isabel waved back and made her way over. They exchanged air kisses.

"It's been forever," Isabel wanted a closer look at the actor. He was thinner than she remembered.

Sam smiled, giving Isabel a once over. "Beautiful as always," he held both of her hands.

"Are you alone?" Isabel wondered.

"I'm waiting for someone. How about you?"

Isabel almost forgot about Jackie. "I'm meeting my daughter."

They both seemed at a loss for words, though they continued holding hands and smiling.

Isabel let go. "What are you doing these days?"

Sam held his smile. Conscious that paparazzi might be near.

Isabel knew he needed work. "You'll get something soon," she encouraged.

"It's that apparent." His expression dropped.

Isabel changed the subject, "The last time I saw you was on Sophie's arm. At my house!"

Sam nodded. "Haven't seen her in forever."

"Sit," Isabel motioned.

They both sat at his table.

Sam pointed over Isabel's shoulder. "Is that your daughter?"

Isabel turned.

"Jackie," she waved to her.

Jackie pointed to the hostess station.

Isabel held up the reservation buzzer that was blinking a single light.

Jackie nodded and moved toward her mother.

Sam stood while Isabel and Jackie hugged.

"I didn't realize you were all grown up," Sam gave Jackie the once over.

Jackie laughed. "Happens."

Isabel gave the introductions. "This is my daughter, Jackie. Jackie, this is Sam. He used to be on Suburb– Listen, we'll wait at the bar. You have someone coming," She couldn't bring herself to mention *that* show.

"It was nice to meet you," Jackie waved as they walked away.

A waiter passed with a plate of sushi and broiled salmon.

Jackie held her stomach and turned away from her mother as the pair continued to weave their way through the outdoor tables.

"Glad you got here when you did," Isabel laughed.

Jackie couldn't say a thing, she was doing everything she could to quell the bile that was rising in her throat.

Isabel noticed Jackie was pale. She placed the buzzer on the hostess stand and grabbed Jackie by the hand. They moved quickly to a small alley, out of sight of the patrons and staff.

Jackie hurled the contents of her stomach against the brick wall.

"Are you okay?" Isabel hadn't seen Jackie ill in years.

Jackie heaved again and handed her mother her bag. "Need a tissue..."

Isabel scrambled. She couldn't find one in her own purse so she opened Jackie's and rummaged through the bag. Her eyes came to rest on the positive test stick in the side pocket.

That's why.

Jackie placed both palms on the wall and leaned over. She didn't think she had anything left to purge.

"Found a Starbucks napkin," Isabel produced the prized paper linen.

Jackie wiped her mouth.

"I guess lunch is off?" Isabel zipped up Jackie's bag.

"Actually, I feel much better." Jackie motioned for Isabel to hand her the bag, then realized her mother had seen the entire contents.

"We'll go somewhere else." Isabel knew Jackie knew that *she* knew. "Maybe we could go home and let Carmen make some lunch."

"You saw the test strip," Jackie sighed.

"Yes." Isabel wasn't certain how to feel, realizing she was going to be a grandmother.

"Are you happy?" Jackie waited for it to sink in.

"Of course," Isabel hugged her daughter. In reality she was numb.

Was she grandmother material?

Jackie was thankful. "That's a relief. We can set a date for the wedding now."

Isabel paused. "Wow. OK, I was just letting the baby news settle in. Why rush into marriage?"

Jackie's mouth dropped. "I'm not rushing. We already had plans."

"Have a big wedding after the baby's born."

"NO!" Jackie didn't follow her mother's logic. "Josh and I are already engaged." She showed her mother the ring. She wore it today to tell her mother the news.

Isabel was not completely surprised, but not expecting all of this at once.

"When did this happen?"

"The baby? Over two months ago, but we weren't trying. The engagement, a few weeks ago." Jackie realized they needed to move out of the alley.

"Why did you keep this from me?" Isabel suddenly caught a whiff of the vomit.

Jackie could see her mother was not totally happy. "I'm sorry. I thought you'd set up a photo shoot with People magazine if we told you we were engaged."

Isabel liked the idea.

"Don't even think about it," Jackie warned.

"Does anyone else know?" Isabel feared the worst.

"Evan knows, because he's helping me with wedding ideas."

Isabel was relieved. She didn't want to be second to Joanne. "Okay, but you were eventually going to consult me, right? I'm paying for it."

Isabel realized at that moment she hadn't told Lyle about Carmen's concern for Joanne. She wouldn't tell Jackie. A mother-to-be didn't need this negative information. It's not like the Mexicans were after any of *them*.

Jackie hugged her mother. "Of course."

She couldn't believe Isabel had taken it so well.

Humberto stood cuffed, hands behind his back. Wakes jammed his baton into Humberto's gut. "Doing you a favor, brother," he whispered.

The guard's halitosis invaded Humberto's nostrils.

"Gallo's people are watching my family. You best find a way to move them back or we're done."

Humberto looked across the aisle and saw his enemies watching from their cells. He respected Wakes. He expected no less from a man responsible for maiming and injuring many hardcore inmates in COR.

Humberto coughed up a wad of phlegm and chucked it at Wakes' badge. The wad hit square in the star and dripped down the medal.

"Fucking shit," Wakes whooped and hollered, high-stepping in rapid succession.

His fellow guards grinned.

Wakes was off the chain!

Wake's complexion turned hot pink in color. The veins in his neck bulging out of his starched collar.

There was no way around this. Vasquez braced himself.

Wakes paused. Then wound up his baton like a World Series batter with bases loaded.

Crack.

Humberto's eyes recognized what had happened almost as fast as his body let go.

Newton's second law of motion: Mass times acceleration.

The baton hit the Colombian's skull in the left temple, causing blood to spew out of the cartel leader's left ear. Humberto flew backwards. His head slammed against the cement wall.

Wakes felt good. "Home run! Get this pile of shit in his cell!"

The guards laughed, grabbed Humberto's feet and dragged him into his cell. They flipped him on his stomach, uncuffing him and leaving him on the floor.

Wakes watched, hands behind his head.

He hadn't planned this. Fucking Vasquez left him no option.

Humberto's cellmate Joachim was on the top bunk reading an auto parts catalog. He sat up on his elbow and assessed the scene.

Humberto didn't move. Blood dotted the floor where his ear exploded.

The cell door slid and hesitated, hovered a moment.

The guards pointed their batons at Joachim in warning.

The inmate didn't move. He watched.

The door finally slammed tight.

The guards moved swiftly to join Wakes.

Joachim jumped down and shook Humberto. "Hey. You alive, man?"

Humberto could hear muffled sounds. He looked at the cement floor, he wasn't certain where he was.

Joachim said a prayer in Spanish, made the sign of the cross and jumped back into his bunk.

Isabel was running late. She'd stopped at Trader Joe's for a few items for a client meeting.

She hoped they would win over recently divorced actress Sally Martindale, who was suing her ex-husband/producing partner for unpaid alimony and business expenses.

Becky loaded the office dishwasher.

Isabel dropped the bags for her to restock the pantry.

"I see Lyle is in," Isabel paused. She noticed the smell of sour wine. "Did someone spill something?"

Becky began unpacking the grocery bags. "He is? And yes, I just mopped the kitchen. I'm not sure who had the party."

"His car is in the lot," Isabel washed her hands and grabbed her purse. "I'll check and see if he has everything prepared. Make a tray with the prosciutto. Roll some with asparagus, cherry tomatoes and mozzarella. And spray some air freshener!"

Isabel move into her office and found her desk was cleared off and smudged. Her pictures and accessories were tossed on the floor.

She unlocked her desk to see if someone had broken in. Nothing was out of place. She locked her purse inside, moving quickly toward Lyle's adjoining office.

"Lyle," she turned the doorknob. "Someone has been in..."

She took a deep breath.

Lyle was naked, flat on his back on the floor and snoring. The woman passed out beside him wore only jeweled spike heels.

Isabel stormed over.

"LYLE!" Isabel stomped her foot near his head.

The woman startled awake, sitting up. "Jesus, Isabel."

It was Melody Mars.

Lyle snored louder.

Melody slapped his dick. "Get up."

"OH!" He grabbed himself and rolled toward Melody, laughing, "You want it."

"Fucking clients!" Isabel screeched.

Lyle blinked several times, coming into focus on his wife.

"She fucked me," Lyle shouted back at her.

Melody laughed. "Lyle was just keeping me company. Robbie had the kids and I was bored. I ran into Lyle at the head shop."

Isabel was stunned. She stared at Lyle. "Since when do you smoke dope?"

Lyle rolled over on his stomach and propped himself on his elbows. "Not now, Isabel—Melody, go home."

Melody stood. Her perfect body was an annoyance to Isabel. She grabbed her shift dress and threw it on. "It was a harmless fuck. He pulled out."

Isabel wanted to slap her. "Am I suppose to thank you both?"

Melody kissed Isabel on the cheek. "We're all pals. I'm not birthing any old man sperm."

"Hear that Lyle. She thinks you'd produce old babies," Isabel half laughed.

What the hell else was she going to do?

"Fuck you," Lyle stood and placed a throw pillow in front of his penis.

Melody pinched his ass. "Be nice to Isabel."

Isabel crossed her arms and waited for Melody to leave.

Becky passed her on her way into the office, "Hello Ms. Mars."

Isabel's assistant carried a tray with several prosciutto arrangements.

"Is this what you mean?" She held out the platter for Isabel's inspection, then noticed Lyle was naked.

"I'll take that," Lyle reached for the platter with his free hand.

Isabel waved her off. "Perfect. Make more."

Becky walked out and closed the door quietly.

Lyle sat at his desk and began eating the appetizers. "God, I'm hungry."

"What are we going to do?" Isabel remained in her crossed-arms Joanne Crawford stance.

"Nothing," Lyle said. "You signed a prenup. Melody fucked *me*, I didn't pursue her."

Isabel scoffed. "Are there others?"

"I can only hope." He grinned, "Try one."

He held up the tray while she studied him.

He looked ridiculous sitting at his desk naked, eating with his hands.

"We'll reconvene after your 11 o'clock." Isabel turned to leave.

"You're better," Lyle said.

Isabel paused. Her back to him.

He repeated, "You heard me. You're a better lay."

She continued toward the door. "I'll have Becky grab your suits at the cleaners."

Wakes called the infirmary.

"Pick up..." He waited. He answered their specific questions and slammed the phone down.

His fellow guards noted a change. Wakes didn't sound like the showman they were accustomed to.

"Gentlemen, I'm cutting out early," Wakes said. He was stewing.

If the DEA wanted Vasquez... they could pick him up in a body bag for all he cared.

"You feelin' okay?" one of the guards muttered.

They ate tacos at their desks while they watched the security monitors.

"I might be a little under the weather," he took care of the necessary paperwork. Then he chucked his bloodied baton on the desk and left.

CHAPTER EIGHTEEN

Liebold approached his superior. "Wakes threatened to inform Vasquez of our plan."

Liebold's superior, Paul Davis, was near retirement and wanted to finish his last few months with a win. He was thin, short, with a gray flat top and kept his long sleeves rolled at three quarter length. "He's pulling your chain. What sense does that make?"

"Maybe you're right," Liebold agreed. "It seems Wakes has more disdain for us than the cartels."

Davis was nodding and twirling a toothpick from side to side in his mouth, "Actually might work in our favor."

Davis had an interior office, no windows. Charts and wanted posters plastered two walls. A white board and handshake photos on another. The wall behind his desk included an autographed photo of the president and a ridiculous assortment of commendation plaques.

"Let's say Wakes cooperates," Davis continued. "And we get Vasquez out to the show. Vasquez will want to save Manning."

Liebold nodded. "Plus we make him aware we're supplying backup to take out Gallo's people."

"Probably be tickled shitless," Davis spit the gnarled toothpick into the trash. "I can't see a problem. What are we missing?"

Liebold went to the whiteboard and drew out a scenario.

"Ok, so I'm Vasquez," he wrote the name on the whiteboard. "And I'm told by the inmate beater that I'm going to get out.

That's a good day. Because the DEA wants me to wipe out Gallo's people. Super excited." He wrote Gallo on the board and drew circles for cartel members.

"Then I bring Manning to the showdown," he went on, drawing a busty stick figure. "In hopes that I, Humberto Vasquez, will negotiate a deal to take her with me to Colombia. It's my birthday!"

Davis was nodding.

"But—Gallo's loose cannon shoots her in front of me." Liebold drew a big red X over Manning's likeness."

"Who is Gallo's problem child?" Davis asked.

"No clue," Liebold said, erasing the board.

"You made that shit up," Davis rocked in his high back office chair. "If Gallo's got a loose cannon, they aren't bringing him to this party."

"Second scenario, then," Liebold began again. "Vasquez strikes a deal with Gallo's people to save Manning. Gallo's goons agree and offer up Manning to Humberto. BUT, at the last minute they kill Humberto, Manning and half of Vasquez crew on the secluded acreage owned by officer Jeremiah Wakes. Compliments of the DEA."

Liebold takes the red marker and streaks it across the board. "Gallo's organization triples and we've helped."

Davis sighs, "Then it *is* Gallo's birthday. And we have an international incident on American soil with a beloved actress, dead. The president and the agency suffer—Gallo has conquered North America with our assistance."

"Right." Liebold wrote FUCK on the board.

"Will Manning cooperate?" Davis was curious.

"Her charitable foundation's mission is to help missing and exploited women and children." Liebold snapped his fingers suddenly, erasing the board. He wrote MANNING at the top of the board, then drew an arrow down to Vasquez and Gallo. "Maybe we've been thinking about this all wrong."

"I'm not following," Davis got up and moved closer.

"Wakes is going to tell Vasquez that we're setting him up—that makes Wakes a good guy in Humberto's eyes. Plus, Vasquez will think we're providing him an escape with Manning to Colombia, right." Liebold drew a crude map of the United States and then South America, with a line of dashes connecting specifically to Colombia.

Davis grabbed the red marker and wrote Gallo and a circle face with two x's for eyes. "So Vasquez has no problem taking out Gallo's people and traveling to the mother country."

They are both feeling positive.

"Now we have to figure out what will lure Gallo to the deal," Davis drew dollar signs.

"No," Liebold erased the dollar signs. "Gallo's prize is to eliminate Manning in front of Humberto." He put a circle around Manning.

"OK, so our mole will be covering her and we'll make sure she's got a bulletproof vest for the party." Davis liked it.

"But what if the Gallo problem child takes Manning out, thinking the deal is going south?" Liebold was perplexed.

"Stop with the fucking problem child! Our mole will know who to pop—he's living with them. He'll get Manning out of harm's way," Davis was adamant.

"But we still need a prize to get Gallo to the party," Liebold was back to square one.

Davis almost danced a jig. "We tell Gallo that he's going to take out the Vasquez crew! It's their birthday."

Liebold tossed the eraser into the garbage. "Why would Gallo believe the DEA wants him to take out Vasquez's crew?"

Davis' eyes lit up. "Because we're now supporting the rival party at the next election in an effort to show the country how inept the incumbent is."

Liebold gaped. "What the fuck? You want to stab the president in the back?"

Davis laughed. "No, I want Gallo to think that."

"What if our people believe it? A plan to ruin the president?" Liebold wasn't certain he could keep it straight. "A bunch of armed agents not knowing who to shoot?"

Davis smiled. "It could work. Trust me, I'm not leaving the agency without a victory. This is my last hurrah before I move to South Dakota."

"It feels like we're back to an international incident." Liebold didn't like it.

"No," Davis was confident. "Because our mole will tip off Gallo's people that we have his back. That we brought reinforcements. They won't know we're turning the tables on them!"

"Then they'll know our mole is a mole." Liebold was now sure the old man was out of his mind, "How else would Gallo's crew member know so much about the DEA's plans?"

"Then we'll send another mole into COR. You design the charges. He'll get busted and moved near Gallo's suite. He'll tip off Gallo. Wakes will have Humberto ready to fly and I'll work to bring Manning's organization in." Davis grabbed a new toothpick out of his pocket protector. He started chewing, "Are we feeling better?"

Liebold said nothing.

Davis slapped the younger agent on the back. "Relax. It's going to be a cakewalk."

Joanne was glad to be back in Los Angeles.

She still hadn't heard from Rick.

Petty stayed in Rick's room upon their return.

It was awkward having adjoining rooms with Petty in the Florida motel. She understood they had to keep the doors open for him to properly protect her, but she wasn't sure about an ongoing arrangement.

She liked him. But Petty was like the relative who wouldn't leave, even though it was his job to stay.

They drove to the foundation. Entering the parking garage, they noticed a young woman sitting on the hood of a car smoking a cigarette.

As Petty escorted Joanne through the garage, he recognized it was Marnie.

"Finally!" Marnie shouted. The echo resounded off the partial concrete walls. She flicked her clove cigarette to floor.

Joanne didn't recognize the girl.

Petty blocked Joanne as the girl came running toward them. He hoped she wouldn't recognize him with his sunglasses on.

"It's me, Marnie."

She looked sweeter than Joanne expected. A genuine smile on her face.

"I've been here every day wondering when I'd catch you."

Joanne was at a loss for words. She knew Rick didn't trust the young woman.

"Were you in the stairwell before?" Joanne continued walking.

"Stairwell? It was likely that guy in the abductor van over there," Marnie pointed. "He's taking pictures. I'm out here because I can't get in there. No one will talk to me."

Petty radioed Clark.

"I'm harmless," Marnie said. "Chill."

Petty held his hand out for the young woman to back up. Marnie noticed at the anchor tat on his wrist.

Joanne continued moving toward the garage entrance to the office but felt wrong turning her back on the girl.

Marnie kept pace. "Tell Godzilla to back off.

Petty protected Joanne's back.

Marnie figured it out. *The mall security guard?!*

"What the fuck? Joanne, you sent Scrappy-Doo to watch me!?"

Joanne continued toward the door, swiped her card and walked in.

Petty kept his eye on Marnie and the van.

She shot him a bird.

He shot one back and went inside.

Marnie continued to shout obscenities. "I came to do you a favor, Joanne!"

Clark Roberts had immediately contacted LAPD and the garage soon filled with flashing lights. The van driver was arrested. Marnie was given a warning.

Joanne entered her office and slammed the door.

Petty could see her through the interior window.

He decided to give her a little space. He'd wait outside.

She took a deep breath. She really didn't want to hear anything related to Petty... or Marnie. She just wanted to decompress and focus on clients.

Her phone trilled.

She grabbed the receiver, "Joanne Manning."

"Good morning, Joanne. My name is Paul Davis. I'm with the DEA..."

CHAPTER NINETEEN

Ken woke Evan.

"Jackie just called, she wants us to go to Vegas. She said you'd understand. What the hell does that mean?"

Evan raised his head, "Why didn't you let me talk to her?"

"She said for you to call her." Ken was perturbed.

Evan sat up and stretched. He couldn't think after a night of red wine.

Ken stood, grabbed his black satin robe and put it on. "What's with the secrets, Ev? Why doesn't she tell me anything?"

Evan reached over and grabbed the water glass off his bedside table, taking a gulp. When he finished, he held the glass out to Ken. "Could you grab me some Tylenol?"

Ken rolled his eyes. He loved being waited on, but not being asked to reciprocate. He grabbed the glass, "Answer me."

Ken walked into their bathroom and ran the water as he fished around in the medicine cabinet. "We have some Percocet and Vicodin. I might need these."

He found the bottle of Tylenol and took it to Evan. The water glass was near overflowing. Ken's way of saying, *don't ask for more.* He plopped it down beside Ken and spilled a quarter of the water, "Sorry."

Evan didn't bother reacting. This was Ken 101. Always put out, but never above expecting Evan to drop everything and wait on him. Evan shook out a few caplets and swallowed them with the water, emptying the glass.

Ken poked at Evan's throat as he swallowed.

Evan slapped his hand. "Why do you do this?"

"Why are you so grumpy frumpy?" Ken fluffed his pillows and sat straight. He crossed his arms and began the interrogation, "So, what gives, secret agent man?"

Evan shook his head. "No clue."

Ken reached out to slap Evan's chest.

Evan grabbed his wrist, "Could you please..." He didn't want to play or argue.

Ken whispered, "Someone can't handle their wine and I'm supposed to be all quiet..."

Evan closed his eyes. "Could you not?"

Ken grabbed his cellphone and nudged Evan, "Call her back. I want to know."

Evan rubbed his eyes. "Don't you think I should call from my phone if this is a covert operation?"

Ken nodded. "Right!" He got up and left the room calling out, "Where did you leave it?"

Evan could hear Ken rummaging around in the kitchen.

"Since when do you eat sardines?" Ken shouted.

"My phone is not the cupboard," Evan yawned.

"Found it." Ken came back into the bedroom and tossed the phone to his lover.

Evan caught it just shy of smacking his nose. "You need to calm down."

Ken plopped back down beside Evan. "I'll be calm."

Evan put the phone on his bedside table. "I'll call in a few minutes."

"I'm not leaving the room." Ken got under the cover and leaned on his left elbow watching Evan.

"Are you going to talk while I'm on the phone with Jackie?" Evan was serious.

"My lips are sealed." Ken laid flat, crossed his arms over his chest and closed his eyes.

Evan wasn't amused. "I'm serious."

Ken opened one eye, "So am I."

"No poking, prodding or rearranging the furniture... nothing. Sit still." Evan grabbed the phone.

Ken sat up and mocked clapping.

Evan dialed.

She picked up.

"Morning, Jackie," Evan listened as Jackie talked.

Ken motioned for speaker.

Evan shook his head.

Ken moved closer to Evan.

"Ken mentioned Vegas..." Evan listened to Jackie, holding the phone tight to his left ear—away from Ken.

Ken started to whisper, waving his hands.

"We'll be there," Evan slapped his right hand over Ken's mouth.

When Ken tried to protest, Evan rolled over and straddled him, pinning him to bed with his hand still clamped over his mouth.

"Hey, can I call you back?" Evan was calm.

Ken struggled, but gave up.

"Sounds good," Evan said. He closed the call.

Ken immediately slapped Evan on the face.

"Manhandler! Bitch!" Ken rubbed his mouth. "Good thing your ring didn't chip a tooth," he rubbed his fingers over his teeth.

Evan got up and put his robe on. He didn't say a word to Ken.

Ken knew Evan had hit the wall. He'd be lucky if Evan spoke to him over the next few days.

Ken yelled out, "I just wanted to hear. Selfish, bitch!"

Rick Jones got word from Clark Roberts and Bart Petty that Marnie had confronted Joanne in the foundation's parking garage.

An LAPD friend followed up with a courtesy call. Marnie Sikes had done nothing to warrant an arrest. In fact, the young woman bragged she was working with the DEA and an agent named Barry Liebold. The van driver was a member of the Gallo cartel. His vehicle was impounded, and he was sent to lockup, pending transfer to Corcoran.

Rick punched agent Liebold's number into his Nokia cell-phone and waited.

The phone rang. Then went to voicemail.

"Rick Jones Security Agency for Barry Liebold, please call me back at..."

His phone showed an incoming call. Jones picked up.

"Rick Jones speaking."

"You called?" Liebold answered.

"Agent Liebold?" Jones asked.

"It is."

"One of the Gallo cartel was stalking my client. As well, I understand one Marnie Sikes is on your radar, too."

"Again, who are you? Who is your client?" Liebold asked.

"Rick Jones Security. Joanne Manning is my client."

Liebold perked up. "Word travels fast."

"Fill me in," Jones said.

"The DEA needs Joanne Manning's help, regarding Humberto Vasquez."

Rick stopped Liebold. "What about Gallo? And Sikes says she's working with *you*, how does that translate to the DEA needs Joanne Manning?"

Liebold wanted to keep it simple. "I'll get to Gallo. Forget about Sikes for a moment—the details get complicated. The short version is, we'd like Manning to visit Vasquez at Corcoran. We hope to satisfy his curiosity with your client and also possibly engage her foundation in extraditing Vasquez out of the U.S. That way he isn't a threat to her and we gain access to his supply line."

"No can do," Jones stuck a piece of gum in his mouth. "I was there on Mt. Lee the night of... He's a danger to her, women in general and the country. For Christ's sake why would the DEA want to feed his obsession?"

"You wanted to know about Marnie Sikes," Liebold changed the subject. He didn't need Jones' opinion.

Rick chewed his gum rapidly. "You using her, too? She might be his next trafficking victim."

"Vasquez wants to marry Sikes." Liebold waited for Jones reaction.

He could see Marnie wanting fame and excitement. "What's the Gallo part?"

Liebold hesitated. "On the level, off the record. The man they arrested in the parking garage was our mole in the Gallo cartel. Sikes means nothing to us. Vasquez knows the Sikes-Manning connection and he's hoping to use Sikes to talk with Joanne Manning. We're not exactly certain why, but we need his cooperation, so at the very least, if he sees Manning, believes we are sincere in our approach, he'll consider our offer."

Rick didn't believe him, "What offer?"

"It doesn't involve your client," Liebold was frank. "But if Vasquez gets his jollies seeing Manning—while she is in a secure environment, usual prisoner/visitor protocol—we achieve our goal. Bride-to-be Sikes will be there too, so he gets what he's been expecting. Hell, you can bring her yourself, she's your client after all. From there, the DEA takes over the job of seeking Vasquez' cooperation."

Rick knew better, there was always more. "What about Gallo? Why's your mole stalking my client? You said earlier you wanted to engage the foundation in extraditing Vasquez out of the country. To gain access to his supply line. What the fuck does that mean?"

Liebold sighed. "I've said way too much already."

Rick paused. "I don't believe you've said enough. You expect me to deliver Vasquez' last victim and then you set Vasquez free to capture her? Fuck no! And now his rival is tailing her?"

"Well, when you say it like that it sounds terrible. But we're not going to let anything happen to Manning. Trust me," Liebold rubbed his forehead. He needed to get off this call—Davis was signaling to him.

"No, I don't trust you. I'm totally fucked by this Gallo news, for one. And good luck with Sikes—she's well suited for Vasquez. May their prison nuptials be a life sentence with no chance for parole. As for my client, you can count her out," Rick was ready to hang up.

Liebold read the note his superior passed him, he gave Davis a thumbs up.

No time like the present, he might as well share the news with Rick.

"Mr. Jones, you should be aware that Manning has already agreed to see Vasquez." Liebold listened to the click, then a dial tone.

Gallo gathered those within sight. He added some new sign language gestures that only his people understood. With Vasquez in the infirmary and Wakes still out on leave, it might be the ideal time to make their move. They were plotting a break.

The old man wanted to escape to Quebec, to see moose, snow and semi-retire in a cold climate where he could experience winter. He knew heat, humidity and dust, but wanted to experience other seasonal changes.

They agreed to rendezvous at breakfast if the circumstances were right.

CHAPTER TWENTY

Humberto was black and blue on the left side of face. He shuffled his feet as the guards escorted him back to his cell.

Joachim met the cartel leader with a brotherly hug.

The two had barely exchanged words during their incarceration, but Humberto appreciated that someone had his back.

Joachim whispered to Humberto that Gallo was up to something, but the Colombian didn't respond.

Joachim whispered again, this time in Humberto's right ear.

Humberto then realized the degree of his hearing loss. There was a high pitched ringing in his left ear, but he hoped his hearing would return over time.

"I'll be your ears, brother." Joachim nodded.

The two grabbed each others wrists and drew in for a quick clinch.

Humberto agreed.

Neither could let on, lest Gallo's people use it against Humberto.

Isabel wore dark glasses. She wished the whole entourage in first class had done the same. She never understood why airlines hadn't the decency to wrap a curtain around each side of first class—rather than expose them to the coach passenger parade.

Lyle wasn't invited.

Isabel was still mad at him, and she wasn't happy with the idea of a quickie Vegas chapel ceremony for Jackie and Josh, either. But at least Joanne wasn't joining them.

Jackie was much further along than anyone realized. She was four months pregnant and getting fuller by the day.

Jackie had wanted Joanne and Rick to join them, but didn't need the stress of her mother and Joanne in such close quarters. And since she couldn't include Joanne, she didn't allow her mother to invite Aunt Sophie.

Because Aunt Sophie would bring a date... and likely the paparazzi.

Josh was not bothered by anything.

Jackie found herself on an emotional roller coaster—always tired, hungry, sick or extremely needy. She wore a simple white satin maternity dress layered with a thin white crocheted sweater over top. Her sandy locks were pulled into a simple up-do with sprigs of faux baby's breath.

For her borrowed item she wore Isabel's white drip earrings, her blue item a small turquoise cross necklace Evan and Ken gave her. She carried her father's photo as something old, and she figured the baby qualified as something new.

Evan and Ken wore orange and purple Hawaiian shirts with white slacks. Josh wore white slacks and a white western shirt with a turquoise bolo. Greta and Judith wore matching salmon colored linen kaftans to complement Ken and Evan's Hawaiian shirts. And Isabel, ever obstinate, wore a little black dress, flats and pearls.

Jackie and Josh wanted a quirky Elvis themed ceremony, since the big Malibu beach wedding was not happening.

Everyone brought an overnight bag.

This would suffice until they could host a reception with Josh's hospital friends, Joanne and Rick, and Jackie's Field-Hause bosses.

Isabel glanced at Jackie. She sat with bride and groom since she didn't know, nor cared to know, the others.

"Is this a legal ceremony?" She asked her daughter. "Don't you need a California marriage license?"

Josh laughed. "Mother Manning, they marry thousands of people in Vegas. Of course, it's legal."

"Call me, Isabel." She told Josh, "I'm not fond of the mother thing."

"Really?" Jackie started to cry.

"Not you, Jackie." Isabel pushed her sunglasses down her nose and looked at those seated around them. She was satisfied they were all preoccupied. "You know me, I'm businesswoman. Not a ..." She shut up before saying, mother-grandmother type.

Tears streamed down Jackie's face. She turned to Josh, "Can you get me a Sprite. I'm not feeling well."

He kissed a tear away on one cheek. Then wiped the other, "You're going to be the most beautiful bride in the world."

Jackie's nose began to run. Just as Josh pulled a tissue out of his pocket and dabbed her nose she began to heave. He grabbed an airsick back and caught the vomit as it sprayed out, spattering Isabel's glasses and right breast.

"For God's sake," Isabel tore off the glasses.

Jackie cried and threw up again.

Isabel spoke to anyone listening, "I was just caught off guard. It'll be okay."

Evan reached between the seats and offered Isabel his handkerchief.

"No thanks." Isabel pushed his hand back. "I'll just splash some water."

Jackie apologized.

Isabel didn't know why she couldn't muster the maternal reaction that seemed natural to other women. Not that she didn't want to be nurturing.

The flight attendant rushed over.

"Aw. Let's take that." She took the airsickness bag and handed Josh a clean one, offering Jackie a large wet wipe. "Can I get you a ginger ale?"

Jackie nodded. "Please."

Isabel whispered, "I should have brought Carmen. I'm sorry."

Jackie didn't respond. This whole scene made her wonder what kind of mother she would be—given her gene pool.

Rick walked into Joanne's apartment and grabbed Petty off the sofa by his collar. "What the fuck is wrong with you?"

Joanne came out of her bedroom toweling her hair. She was dressed in shorts and t-shirt. "What are you doing?"

"I'm going to tear this piece of shit to shreds for letting you believe it's okay to see Vasquez!" Rick let go of Petty and Bart reeled back on his heels.

Petty pushed back at Rick, then stepped away from his business partner. "She's not seeing Vasquez."

"Actually, I am." Joanne told them both.

Jones felt as if he'd been struck. He got into her face. "Why are we here?"

Joanne backed up, "To protect me, asshole. Not preach to me. You work for me. And quite frankly, Marnie Sikes seems to be a better detective than any of you!"

Petty balked. "You mean Roberts! You and I had just arrived... And by the way, we're not detectives."

Rick was ready to punch him.

Joanne tossed the towel on the sofa. "I want closure with Vasquez, if that's okay with you two? The DEA has assured my safety."

That word again, Rick's jaw pulsed. *Closure...* Then what? The Colombian wasn't interested in Joanne's ability to heal and move on—she had to know that much already. He held both his hands in front of her, like he wanted to grab her.

She moved away from him.

Petty got between them.

"Back up, Rick. You're out of line, man."

Rick tried again, "What did you agree to, Joanne?"

"That I would visit him at the prison. I'm not sure what he'll say... or what I'll say." Joanne grabbed her towel again and thought about throwing it at Rick. "But I'm sick of running. At the very least, my work at the foundation requires me to do something. Do you have any idea how many lives could be saved if he and I could reach some sort of agreement? Because I do, I can give you a figure."

Petty suddenly realized Joanne blindsided him. "When did you talk to the DEA?"

"After we ran into Marnie in the garage." Joanne thought they were overreacting.

"FUCK!" Petty screamed.

She ignored him. "An agent named Paul Davis asked if I would accompany agent Barry Liebold to the prison next Friday."

Jones looked at Petty. They seemed to have an understanding.

"Joanne," Rick was patient. "You can't make any other arrangements like this without consulting us. I now have to hire backup."

"I'll pay for it. After the Vasquez visit I want to be free of all this fear and anxiety. Live like a normal person." Joanne teared up, "Cancel your services."

Rick was stunned.

Petty noted Jones' wounded demeanor.

A long silence passed before Rick said, "No other arrangements, or I'll cancel services."

He waited for her to respond.

She nodded in agreement.

Wakes watched the security cameras. He'd taken all of his sick days and moved his wife and kids to a quiet town in Connecticut, far from anyone or anything associated with either of their families.

If the Vasquez or Gallo crews were watching the Wakes family, they made themselves unknown.

Wakes promised his wife he'd be back once he struck a deal with the DEA. He wanted protection. He'd served the community and the victims who'd been violated by the criminals in COR. He knew his rage was not justified, but he also knew that he was no worse than the people he associated with daily.

Isabel waved for Carmen to stop the vacuum.

Carmen turned the machine off and clapped her hands together, "Welcome back. So happy Meez Isabel will be a grandmama."

Isabel rolled her eyes.

Carmen went to hug Isabel. "Meez Jackie will be a good mama."

Isabel ignored Carmen. Instead she pointed to the entryway, "You missed a spot. Lyle must have tracked something in on his golf shoes.

Carmen's eyes got big. "No. Mister Lyle not here."

"Then you tracked it in," Isabel accused.

Carmen made the sign of the cross. "I come in the back."

Isabel threw her hands up. "Just clean it."

Carmen held a finger to her lips. She whispered, "Did you tell Mr. Lyle about Miss Joanne."

Isabel didn't follow. "What about Joanne? Are you stalling?"

Carmen whispered again, "The Mexican mafia?"

Isabel's eyes got big. She'd forgotten all about Carmen's concern. She whispered back, "They followed you into the house?"

Carmen shook her head no, crossed herself again and looked up. "God forgive Meez Isabel. Please send the angels and saints to Miss Joanne."

Isabel tugged at the maid's sleeve. "How about to Isabel, too."

Carmen started praying in Spanish.

"Ladies," A male voice interrupted.

They both screamed. Carmen held her chest.

Lyle laughed. "What are you two afraid of?"

Isabel slapped the maid's arm. "It was Lyle."

Carmen nodded. Tears of joy filled her eyes, "Thank you, Jesus."

Lyle dug his hands into his pockets. "Jesus, hmm."

Isabel huffed, "Carmen thinks her cousin in the Mexican mafia is after Joanne. And that he broke in. That's who we thought you were."

Lyle didn't follow.

"Here?" He looked around.

Carmen gasped, "Not my cousin. Not my family." She made another sign of the cross.

Lyle shook his head. "Why would they come here if they want Joanne?'

Isabel threw her head back, "I don't know. Carmen?"

They both turned to the maid.

"A friend of a friend of my cousin heard someone mention Miss Joanne is in danger," Carmen whispered.

"Carmen, you are confused. Vasquez is Colombian," Lyle laughed, keeping his speech slow and watching for signs of recognition from her. "He is the one who was arrested. Plus, Joanne has a bodyguard. Do not worry about her."

Carmen shook her head. "No. No. No. Mr. Lyle. The Colombians and Mexicans are in the same prison. They don't like each other."

Lyle thought about it. "You're saying the rival gang is watching Joanne?"

Carmen nodded.

Isabel didn't follow.

"Can she get back to vacuuming? You tracked in dirt..." She pointed to the entryway.

Lyle turned. "I came in through the garage."

Carmen collapsed.

CHAPTER TWENTY-ONE

"Do we call the police?" Isabel knelt down and shook Carmen.

"And say what?" Lyle was still unclear on Carmen's fear.

They heard footsteps.

Isabel got up and grabbed Lyle's hand and pulled him into the hallway.

"Oh my God, Carmen!" Becky knelt down to wake Carmen.

Isabel sighed. "How long have you been here?"

"Fifteen or twenty minutes?" Becky felt Carmen's pulse.

Isabel gave Carmen a soft slap on the face. "Wake up, it's just Becky."

Carmen slowly opened her eyes. She was confused.

Lyle towered over the maid.

"You're fine," he shouted. "The ladies have this under control. I'll make my own martini."

He left the room.

Isabel pointed at Becky, "You scared Carmen. She didn't see you come in."

"I took Jackie's wedding gifts to the den, like you asked." Becky helped Carmen sit up. "I tried to get her attention, but she didn't hear me over the vacuum."

"It was Becky," Isabel spoke loudly to Carmen's face. "No one else."

The maid nodded her head.

"Can I get you some water?" Becky asked Carmen.

"She's fine," Isabel insisted. "She needs to finish her work."

Becky ignored Isabel. "I'm getting her a glass of water."

"Carmen can get it herself." Isabel looked to her maid, "You're fine."

Carmen got to her knees, then stood. "I do not feel well."

Becky came back and gave Carmen the water. She drank it down.

Becky walked her to a chair.

"Fine," Isabel said. "You two work it out. I'm joining Lyle for a martini."

Paul Davis briefed Barry Liebold and Rick Jones. They were at a secure location a few miles from Corcoran. An industrial complex the DEA rented for equipment storage and raid acquisitions.

"Thank you for coming," Davis held his hand out to Jones.

They gave each other a firm, challenging grip.

Liebold nodded. "We've got more men watching Gallo's activities, in relation to your client. Our mole assured us that he was the sole stalker for Gallo. He sincerely attempted to provide what the cartel leader wanted and not compromise Manning's safety. In fact, he was keeping tabs on Marnie Sikes, as it relates."

Davis took a sip from his water bottle. "Can I offer you anything?"

Rick shook his head.

"We would like Ms. Manning to wear a wire. So we can review the conversation."

"With surveillance cameras everywhere how's a wire necessary?" Rick didn't see the point.

"It helps us recall voice inflections..." Liebold said.

Rick put a piece of gum in his mouth and chewed. "After she has complied, she's done. Right?"

Davis looked at Liebold.

Rick felt déjà vu coming on. "What?"

"It's hard to say, if there's rapport and a second visit seems beneficial?" Davis nodded to Liebold, who nodded back.

Jones snapped his gum. He no longer knew what Joanne would say. He couldn't speak for her, "Let's get this over with."

"We'll see you here tomorrow." Davis stuck his hand out to Jones again. "We'll get her wired and, as you say, get it over with."

Jones ignored Davis' offer to shake. He didn't trust either of them. "Tomorrow."

Liebold walked Jones to the door. "Wear a raincoat. Forecast is a downpour."

"Downpour," Jones acknowledged and left.

Davis waited until Jones was out of the room. "Agent Gabriel West is now Santiago Ortiz. He's bunking in the cell next to Gallo."

Liebold nodded. "What charges?"

"Possession," said Davis, "We let him in with enough to offer it to Gallo for protection."

"Did it work?" Liebold asked.

"Like a charm," Davis laughed. "Ortiz is playing scared. He's willing to run supply for Gallo."

"Gallo like him?" Liebold was impressed.

Davis grinned, "Like a hot buttered croissant."

"So we let Marnie Sikes walk Manning in, impress Vasquez." Liebold rubbed his chin,

Davis was distracted. "Bring Sikes in. Play it by ear. Everything changes tomorrow, anyway. Control shifts," Davis' phone rang.

Liebold felt Davis was overconfident. "Better watch the weather—smart to suggest a possible second visit."

Davis ignored him, picked up his phone. "Davis here."

Liebold mouthed, "Heading out."

Davis nodded. He covered his phone, "Be ready."

CHAPTER TWENTY-TWO

Rain came down in sheets that resembled a colossal waterfall. The windshield wipers were of no use, but Rick let them fight the deluge anyway. His Hummer moved through the flooding streets without incident.

"Seems fitting weather for a cartel meeting."

Rick didn't expect Joanne would respond. They hadn't been speaking to each other much the last few days.

She tried to focus her thoughts.

A streak of lightning etched across the dark sky, lighting up the prison in the distance. A crack of thunder sent Joanne's hands up.

They passed several abandoned or stalled vehicles on the road side.

"It's like a horror movie." She couldn't believe it was still early afternoon, but it looked like midnight.

"Got that right," Rick muttered, snapping his gum.

Her emotions ranged from anger to fear to apathy. She didn't know how to feel about Vasquez. Paul Davis had wired her an hour earlier. She wondered if the rain would short circuit the device?

Buckets of water streamed down the windshield, only to be replaced by more.

"It'll be over soon," she said to her reflection in the passenger window. She yawned big.

They saw a small figure walking in the rain. It appeared to be female, must have abandoned her vehicle. Joanne insisted they stop, though Rick did so with hesitation—he knew more than one aspect of this operation was beyond his control. He'd like to limit his liabilities.

The woman was soaked and shivering, they could barely see her. She grabbed the handle and opened the back door. She slipped, but managed to pull herself inside the vehicle.

"There's a blanket in the very back," Rick told her, watching from the rearview.

She was shivering uncontrollably. She retrieved the blanket and turned toward them.

It was Marnie Sikes.

Rick didn't like the coincidence—if it was a coincidence.

"It looks like your accomplice has arrived," he said to Joanne.

Joanne turned around. "Marnie?"

Marnie's mascara resembled a racoon's mask. Her lips were purple.

"Thanks for the lift," her teeth chattered.

Joanne had some lukewarm coffee in a styrofoam cup. She handed it to Marnie.

Marnie took it eagerly. She really was a mess.

"What happened to your car?" Rick stopped the Hummer for a moment and unbuckled.

"It just stopped," she shivered.

He took off his windbreaker and passed it back to her, "There's a granola bar in the top pocket, if you're hungry."

He rebuckled and continued toward Corcoran.

"Thanks, man," Marnie's hair was now pixie length. She took off all of her clothes and wore the large windbreaker.

Davis and Liebold greeted Wakes in an interrogation room. They wanted to brief him on the visitation. They shook hands and grabbed a seat on either side of the narrow table.

A crack of lightning caused the lights to flicker.

Wakes didn't move. He glanced around. He sensed something.

"Worst rain we've seen. Think they're coming?" Wakes leaned in. Both hands joined together in a fist, elbows on the table. His large frame slumped to table height.

Davis and Liebold sat back. Confident.

"We were with Jones and Manning shortly before we got there. He's solid. They might be late, but they'll be here," Davis nodded to Liebold.

Liebold nodded to Wakes.

Wakes laughed. "Vasquez is a happy, horny bastard. You'd think it's his birthday."

Davis and Liebold looked at each other. Davis took a toothpick out of his pocket and began to chew. "Our thoughts exactly."

Joanne and Marnie stayed in the Hummer.

Rick couldn't leave the car running, he didn't trust Marnie. He wanted to check on their arrangements before leading Joanne in.

"What do you hope to accomplish in seeing Vasquez?" Joanne asked Marnie.

Marnie was wringing out her clothes as water spilled on the vinyl floor.

"I might ask you the same thing," Marnie was curt. She rummaged through Rick's windbreaker and found a $100 bill and the granola bar. She pulled her slacks on and stuffed the bill in the soaked pocket. She struggled to get the wet top back on, then tore open the granola bar and began to eat.

Joanne was annoyed. She remembered how Jackie tried to keep up their friendship even when Marnie was acting bizarre. She wondered if the wire was picking them up now?

"I'm hoping the cartel will stop trafficking innocent women," Joanne answered.

Marnie laughed, a guttural chuckle. "And you're just the one to get it done," she clapped.

Joanne looked at the lightning in the distance. Prepared for the thunderclap.

BOOM!

"Jesus," Marnie jumped.

Joanne unbuckled herself and turned to get a better look at Marnie.

"If you expect to deliver me and win your place in Humberto Vasquez's heart, you better start acting like it. I have nothing to lose by leaving, but it sounds like you do." She studied the girl's face. She began to wonder what the point was.

Marnie nodded. "Go, Joanne! And I'm not mocking you. It's about time you showed some guts."

Joanne took a deep breath and turned around. She imagined Marnie choking her from behind.

The driver's door opened. Rick jumped in, soaking the driver's side.

"They're ready."

Marnie squealed, "Showtime!"

Joanne felt sick to her stomach. She had no idea why. After all, it was a secure facility and they would be behind a glass partition. Plus, Rick would be there.

Rick looked at Joanne. She looked pale.

He checked Marnie in the rearview. Even in smudged makeup, she looked exuberant.

"Let's roll," Rick snapped his gum.

He wasn't taking Marnie anywhere after the visitation. The DEA could have her.

CHAPTER TWENTY-THREE

Jackie and Josh stretched out on their living room sofa bed. It was becoming their tradition to watch videos when Josh came home from working long hours.

Jackie nibbled at her popcorn, feeding Josh several kernels.

"Why do they call this Life Is Beautiful? It's so sad," she rubbed her tears.

A crack of lightning shut the power off. She screamed.

Josh rolled toward her, "Your wish is my command."

"I hope mother or Joanne aren't driving in this," Jackie got fearful. "We still haven't told Joanne we're married or pregnant."

Josh hugged her close. "We will. We have a lot of people to tell."

Jackie nuzzled him back. "I don't want to watch that movie when the power comes back. I don't want to be thinking about a child or a parent..."

He kissed her neck. Then her cheek.

Jackie grabbed the throw they had over them and rubbed her nose.

Josh rubbed her belly. "We'll tape Sesame Street for the baby and watch that."

"Do you think we're having a boy or a girl?" Jackie placed her hand on his. "I think we're having a boy."

"And I think we're having a girl."

"Is that a medical opinion?" She was serious.

"Yes. I forgot to tell you, I have x-ray vision." Josh pinched her nipple.

"That hurt!" She slapped him, "Why did you do that?"

"They're getting big. It's kind of sexy." He leaned in to kiss her. She pushed him away.

He moved in to the curve of her neck, running his tongue up to her ear.

She giggled.

Another crack of lightning. The lights came on and the television flickered.

Josh quickly turned off the TV and lamp.

"Where were we..." He resumed kissing his bride.

Joanne and Marnie sat side by side as Humberto was brought in.

He was a towering figure. His long black hair pulled back in a ponytail. His prison blue uniform accentuated the lean lines of his biceps and pectoral muscles.

He made eye contact with Joanne. He was mesmerized.

He sat, grabbing the phone receiver.

Marnie waved to him, as if to say, "I did it."

She was still damp but had freshened up in the ladies' room, drying her clothes with the hand dryer. She picked up the phone.

"Humby!" She squealed. "I know you want to talk with Joanne..."

"Yes!" he commanded. "Put her on."

Rick and Davis stood by the door in the background. Watching.

Marnie happily handed Joanne the receiver.

Gallo had a visitor a few stations down. He couldn't believe his eyes.

Joanne took a deep breath. She remembered Vasquez from Mt. Lee. He had the same animalistic expression as he did that night, only he was bigger now and much more menacing. She raised the phone toward her ear.

Lightning splintered in a sizzling heat and seemed to explode just outside the building. She jumped and an involuntary scream escaped her. She dropped the receiver.

Her startled expression excited him. He wanted to hold her, feel her. He was transfixed.

She grabbed the phone and listened.

Humberto was reassuring. "Marquel. You are as beautiful as..."

The sound cut out and she couldn't hear him.

Joanne turned to Rick, reassuring herself of his presence—he and Liebold had the windowless entry door open, Rick appeared concerned with the door itself. He nodded to her, then stepped over the threshold with Liebold leaning out behind him, pointing. She turned back to Vasquez.

A buzzing sound rippled across the sound system. The guard behind Humberto turned to his left and right quickly, looking disturbed.

Joanne pulled the phone away and started to look for Rick again when another crack of lightning shocked her. The lights flickered, a door slammed. The phone was smoking in her hand and she became aware of an aching sensation in her palm.

Even Marnie seemed worried, which caused Joanne to drop the phone. She started to feel like she was in a bad dream and she tried to remind herself of the reason she was there.

Vasquez was on his feet. He appeared to move in slow motion as he punched the guard behind him. The guard dropped in a couple of flashes of light. Humberto took the guard's weapon, turning to Jeremiah Wakes.

He fired several shots into Wakes' chest and neck. One of the bullets passed through Wakes' neck, hitting another inmate.

The power surge strobed the lights and the alarm sound was a deafening beep that pulsed relentlessly. Joanne was paralyzed for a moment, unable to recognize what was happening.

An echo reverberated through the building as all the cell doors in their wing rolled in a grinding symphonic whine, crashing opened. Another buzzer sounded an alarm as the doors remained stuck in an open position.

Whooping and calling was followed by the stampede of hundreds of men.

Joanne couldn't see Rick amongst the bodies and flashing lights. Visitors screamed, running for the exit only to disappear in the crush of charging prisoners.

The loudspeaker tried to compete with the alarms, "Do ... leave... area ... will get hurt."

The electric gates opened and shut in short bursts.

Gunfire was heard.

Joanne blinked a few times. She saw Marnie run, but she remained, paralyzed in her seat.

She watched as several prisoners came into possession of police-issued weapons, holding guards hostage as reinforcements from other COR units descended on the building. She had to move... but where? She could see nothing but smoke, blue-uniformed bodies and chaos descending around her.

Finally she crawled under the small counter she and Marnie had been sitting it, under the visitation window.

The lights went black and more screams followed. The only illumination came from the prisoners' side of the glass.

Joanne felt someone take her hand, pulling her out of the melee.

Rick?

The strobing continued behind her. She couldn't see where she was going.

She could smell smoke. She assumed a fire had broken out in the cells. She couldn't see who had her hand. She just trusted that whoever it was, they were bringing her to a better place.

As they moved through an unfamiliar doorway, she noticed the older man's blue prison attire. She needed to separate from whoever this was. She pulled back.

"You'll die in there," he screamed. "You'll be raped once they take control."

He dragged her by the wrist, running as fast as he could outside, though he was having a hard time breathing.

The lights from the guard towers sliced through their path. She realized this prisoner had been shot.

Shots rang from all directions. The guard tower and the yards.

More screams continued as police helicopters held their search lights on the ditches and roads. More shots could be heard in the distance.

The prisoner holding on to Joanne pulled her down to the parking lot's rain saturated asphalt surface. He rested there, groaning. He was losing blood.

Joanne fell to her knees. She was grateful for the older man's assistance. She couldn't see Rick or the Hummer among the police lights. Barricades were being erected before them.

"Thank you," she shouted to the man. "You need help."

The man nodded.

Police called out to Joanne on a bullhorn. They had a gun trained on the man.

"Ma'am. Are you okay?" the bullhorn squealed.

Her clothing was smeared in his blood.

"Yes," she shouted. "He saved my life."

Though she doubted they heard her.

Two officers jogged over and held a flashlight on the man's face.

"Juan Carlos Gallo, located, down," one officer spoke into his shoulder radio.

"Can you help him?" Joanne begged.

"He'll be tended to along with hundreds of others."

Gallo gasped for air.

Joanne spoke in his ear. "I don't know who you are, Mr. Gallo. But thank you..."

Gallo smiled. He tried to speak.

She put her ear to his mouth.

"Seeing the moose," he muttered. She watched as he closed his eyes.

She couldn't have heard him correctly?

The police were escorting her away.

She reached into her blouse and ripped off the wires, tossing them on the ground. Another crack of lightning lit up the sky.

The rain slowed.

"I came here with two other people, how do I find them?" She asked the officer.

He recognized her. "You're that actress!"

"I was," she shouted back. "I need to find Rick Jones!"

They escorted her toward a media truck that was setting up tarps. "You'll be safe here," the officer said, letting her go.

Sure, she thought. Though this may be the one time the media were the best option.

Where was Rick? He had to be out here somewhere.

He had to be, she told herself again and again.

A reporter on the scene was dumbfounded but thrilled to see Joanne Manning.

"Would you give us an eyewitness account for the live remote?"

CHAPTER TWENTY-FOUR

Sophie was drunk before Isabel arrived. She was in rare form now, catching herself as she stumbled into her sunken living room.

"Almost rolled an ankle." She put the refilled pitcher on a narrow sofa table, holding on to her glass with one hand and the furniture with the other.

"I didn't know Lyle had it in him," Sophie chuckled, pouring Isabel another martini. She belched, "What on earth did Melody see in him? You've had too many now. You can't drive, honey."

Isabel laughed. "I'm a better lay. He said so."

Sophie clanged her glass against Isabel's. "Old broads. We can fuck 'em."

Isabel tossed her drink back and felt the room move.

The television was on mute. Sophie's eyes got big. She pointed, still trying to steady herself. She knew once she sat down she wouldn't be getting up again for awhile.

Isabel turned to see Joanne on the large TV. Her name was on the bottom of the screen below the video feed. "Christ! What's... she doing now?!"

Sophie unmuted the television.

They both stared in astonishment as Joanne shared from her perspective how the storms caused the prison electrical system to jam, leaving all the cell doors open. Panic, riots and electrical fires ensued. She had discovered that she was actually saved by the leader of the Mexican Mafia—who helped her in his own attempt to escape.

"Carmen's cousin," Isabel slurred.

Sophie cut her off, "Shh."

The reporter asked Manning, "Why were you at the prison?"

Joanne tried to keep her answers short. "To see Humberto Vasquez."

The reporter's mind was clearly blown. "He is in prison for attempting to kidnap you, along with drug and human trafficking charges."

Joanne nodded.

Sophie cackled. "Oh my God, did you see his face? The station is chinking the register... What a fucking interview! Oh, that reminds me, I should call Javier."

Isabel scowled.

The reporter continued, "Aren't you afraid Vasquez has escaped and could attempt to kidnap you again?"

Sophie gasped. "Hadn't... thought... of that," she hiccupped.

Isabel held her glass up. Sophie poured them both a refill.

"He may have died," Joanne didn't want to make light of all the lives that were impacted.

The reporter nodded and turned to the camera. "To the residents of Corcoran, California, it is advised to lock your doors and stay inside. There is a massive manhunt as we speak for all the inmates who escaped this section of the correction facility. The authorities tell us the body count and missing may take weeks to assess—" he turned to acknowledge Joanne as he spoke "—the identities of those who perished," he pointed to the building, "in what is still a blazing fire. And as Ms. Manning just said, it appears a computer failure and electrical outage have challenged the prison's locking mechanisms, among other things. No word yet as to whether or not the prison's computerized files may have been erased, or if other buildings on the campus have also been compromised. It is confirmed, however, that Charles Manson and Sirhan Sirhan are not prisoners in this section. They remain in lockdown, as far as we know..."

Joanne wondered where Rick was. She couldn't fathom how all the law enforcement and media on the ground had responded so quickly in this weather. The Hummer was nowhere to be seen, she had to hope it was Rick who had been behind the wheel when it left.

The reporter turned back to Joanne. "If Vasquez is out there and can see this right now, what would you say to him?"

Joanne turned toward camera. "Humberto Vasquez, please release the women and minors you've captured through human trafficking. The Marquel Foundation is dedicated to bringing these victims home. Our law enforcement partners seek your cooperation."

The reporter touched his ear piece, "I'm being told we should move inside to follow some developing stories."

Sophie plopped down on an overstuffed chair. "Joanne is the best drama on television!"

"Bitch," Isabel mumbled, waving Sophie off. "Back to me. I'm gettin... a divorce."

"The prenup?" Sophie used her glass to draw a question mark in the air. She wore most of her drink in the gesture, she lamented, "Damn waste."

They both laughed much longer than necessary.

"Talent manage..." Isabel closed her eyes.

Sophie couldn't focus. She tried to turn the television off by blinking her eyes, then began to snore.

Humberto looked out the motel curtain. He was shirtless and still wearing his mud caked prison issued pants.

Marnie sat on the toilet with the bathroom door open watching Humberto pace like a caged lion.

"No one knows we're here. Relax!" She shouted.

In their escape from COR they managed to start her vehicle and get ahead of SWAT and the media. She'd checked into the roadside motel not twenty minutes earlier—the owner was barely awake. He took her hundred and gave her forty back, saying he would give her another thirty when he could make change, if she only stayed one night. Her gave her the key.

The fact that she was covered in mud didn't seem to faze him.

"Shut up," Humberto commanded.

Marnie flushed the toilet and joined him in the bedroom.

She was down to her bra and underwear. They both needed a shower.

Humberto turned from the window. "Do you have anything?"

Marnie danced over to him and dropped her bra. "I've got weed."

He reached into her panties.

She tried to kiss him, but he pushed her on the bed.

"Where's the weed," he demanded.

"In my bag."

He grabbed her shoulder bag off the table and found a packed pipe and lighter in a zip-lock baggie. He lit the bowl and inhaled deeply.

She crawled to the end of the bed toward him and took off her panties.

"While you have your mouth around that," she began tugging at his pants. "I'll get my mouth around this."

The caked dirt crumbled off his pants onto the matted shag rug.

He took another hit.

Marnie got to her knees and began working to get Humberto erect.

"Seems a guy who just broke out of prison would be harder," she teased, sucking.

He grabbed her by the hair and put the pipe to her lips.

She took a big hit then sat back on her heels, lightheaded. "It's some good shit."

He began masturbating and then gave her a mouthful of his dick to work on.

He closed his eyes. This was Joanne pleasuring him.

He picked her up and moved onto the bed. He mounted her, keeping his eyes closed.

This was Joanne. He loved the way she felt.

Marnie stroked his chest and groaned encouragingly.

He drove into her faster, thinking about what their life in Colombia would like.

Marnie loved his rhythm. She watched his concentration as he moved deeper.

"My God," he climaxed suddenly.

She was ecstatic.

He was content. Satisfied.

He shuddered again. Then stayed with her a moment longer and rolled away.

Marnie crawled from the bed and grabbed the pipe off the table, lighting it.

She inhaled deeply and handed it back to him.

"Let's do it again," she suggested.

He took a hit.

"It's good stuff, right?"

She took the pipe back and inhaled as he exhaled.

"Where did you get this?"

"Some Mexican dude near the jail."

Humberto grabbed her by the throat. "What Mexican?"

Marnie gasped and hit at him, trying to pry his hands off.

He let her go.

"What the fuck is wrong with you?" She coughed, "Are you insane?"

He threw the pipe at the wall.

"That's mine," Marnie slapped at him.

He brought his hand hard across her face, then got up and went to the bathroom.

Her face hurt. She felt dizzy. She walked over to the dresser mirror.

She was high, but it still hurt. His hand print made her eye twitch.

"What gives?" Marnie screamed.

"I want to clean *you* off of me." Humberto started the shower. He left the door open. Steam quickly fogged the bathroom mirror.

"Um, that's fucking rude," she shouted, marching into the bathroom.

She got in the tub with him, not bothering to wait for his permission.

He soaped up his long hair and looked down at her sad red face. She stood there watching him.

"I'm going to find Joanne now that I am free. I have you to thank." He continued to soap his chest and stomach.

"What's wrong with *me*?" She hoped he was just playing with her. She needed him to care.

He held his head under the water.

"You said you wanted to marry me, remember?" Marnie slapped his chest with both hands. "Remember?"

He laughed. "Why would I marry you, Marnie? You are a child."

She didn't want to cry. "You used me."

"I'll take care of you." He laughed again, "You girls are all alike."

Marnie got out, dripping. That was it. She didn't need this shit. She went into the bedroom and grabbed her bag. She found a metal nail file and marched back into the bathroom.

She pulled the curtain back. He was washing his face, eyes closed.

"No Humberto, I'm not like any other woman you know."

She stabbed him in the scrotum.

He screamed and grabbed for her.

She stepped back. He placed his hand over his testicles and wailed.

She lunged again, aiming for his left thigh—the femoral artery.

"No!" he moaned.

Blood gushed. He grabbed his thigh to stop the blood and slipped on the soap. This time she caught him in the gut as he fell on his face and more blood gushed out of his broken nose.

She closed the shower curtain and let the water wash over him.

He was unconscious, losing blood rapidly.

She climbed onto the edge of the tub, straddling him and letting the shower head rinse his blood off her naked body. She left the shower running as he bled out, face down in the mildewed-tile corner.

She spat. "Some fucking bad ass you turned out to be."

She left the bathroom, finding some change in her bag. She was still high, and now she was tired and hungry.

She slipped her tee on and her panties, grabbing the room key on her way out the door. She dripped as she walked barefoot across the faded gray walkway, her clean feet making wet prints on the dusty surface.

The Coke machine blinked and hissed. She slammed her coins into the soda machine and the Coke can clanged to the bottom.

The other vending machine had a few sun-scorched junk food items dangling on the edge of its spiral bins. She kicked at it and saw a mouse dive down behind the drop slot.

"Mine, fucker!" She said to the rodent.

She got her arm up into machine far enough to shake the chewed package of peanut butter crackers loose.

A bored traveler stood in his open doorway and spoke. He'd watched Marnie pass his darkened doorway.

She turned, not hearing what he'd said. "Pardon me?"

"There was a riot at the prison a few hours ago," the figure took a drag from his cigarette and flicked it into the parking lot. "Sounds like pandemonium. Keep your door locked."

She handed him the can, showing him her chewed nails. "You mind?"

He popped the top and handed it back to her, noticing the bruise starting to form on her cheek.

She took a long gulp of the soda.

"God that tastes good," she lingered there for a moment, eying the guy.

He looked like an insurance salesman.

"Thanks," she started back to her room.

"You heard me," he said.

"Right!" She held up the soda can as she walked away, "Prisoners on the loose."

He watched her square the key and move into her room without further acknowledgment.

He took her for a battered wife. Seemed to be alone, which was probably a good thing. He hoped to hell she was making a clean break.

Marnie held the cold can to her cheek. She turned on the TV and watched an infomercial, assessing the room. She took off her shirt and picked up the remains of her muddy clothes.

The tub was overflowing. She saw ponding on the bathroom floor.

Her feet sloshed through pink liquid and she shut the shower off.

She washed her clothes in the bathroom sink and hung them to dry on the shower curtain rod over Humberto's body. His foot was blocking the drain, so she reached down and moved it.

The water went down rapidly.

Afterward, she found her pipe and smoked another bowl.

She finished the crackers. Then she put out the "Do not disturb" sign, got under the sheets and proceeded to watch reruns of *Saved By The Bell*.

CHAPTER TWENTY-FIVE

Davis and Liebold were lucky to find shelter in a SHU in the next building where the guards and inmates were locked down.

Liebold said to Davis, "If Gallo and Vasquez got out alive, they're heading home. We're back to square one."

Davis chewed his toothpick. "Yep. And I retire a happy man. They'll be your headache."

Liebold nodded. "How will this affect the election?"

"The prison break is state issue. The president will be fine," Davis stretched out on a cement cot. "Wonder why the inmates complain about this? It feels fine to me."

Lou Bartalow read the newspaper headline:

VASQUEZ DEAD. GORED BODY FOUND IN MOTEL NEAR PRISON.

He read a few more lines and was floored to see Marnie Sikes' name as a person of interest—apparently she'd been visiting Vasquez in Corcoran.

Lou grabbed his cellphone and scrolled through his contacts. He called Jim Sikes.

Sikes answered. Annoyed, "You read the paper. Seems everyone wants to catch up."

Lou understood.

"Media is in front of my house and my office," Sikes complained.

"Hey Jim, I'm sorry. I don't suppose you've heard from her?" Lou was apologetic, "Anything I can do?"

"Is it true you're running Joanne's foundation?"

"I oversee the admin. Why?"

"Any way to make this look like Marnie was working with Joanne?" Sikes was desperate. He hadn't communicated with his daughter in months and hadn't had much to say to her after she was busted at Isabel's house. He had no idea what the hell his daughter was doing... "I mean, they were there on the same day, right?"

Lou hesitated. It suddenly dawned on him that he was the common denominator in Vasquez' entry into the states. The cartel leader was in a California prison as a result—where Marnie decided to contact him for some reason. FUCK!

"I can't," Lou finally said. He hated to turn anyone down.

"It was worth a try."

Lou couldn't think of any words to console his old friend.

Sikes sighed. "I've canceled my office appointments. Just hoping the women going into labor this week aren't readers."

Lou thought about Zach. At least his friend could finally rest in peace. He didn't want Sikes to break down. "I'd ask you to play a round of golf, but we'd probably be discovered."

Sikes half laughed and wanted to cry. "I deliver babies, Lou. I think about when Marnie was little, I don't know what happened. I don't know where she is..." He couldn't talk.

CHAPTER TWENTY-SIX

Rick approached from Joanne's office doorway.
She was stunned. Angry, floored... but also happy to see him.

No one had heard from him in months.

"We all feared the worst," Joanne stayed seated at her desk.

Which was true, but somehow Petty had been able to reassure her he had to be out there somewhere. She felt it too, but couldn't explain it. She just knew she couldn't lose him too...

He was noticeably thinner, tired.

She'd worked at the foundation every day since the prison incident.

Donations were up. Hotline tips and offers were pouring in.

She figured if the paparazzi were following her it may as well be where she could do some good.

Clark Roberts poked his head in, "Have you told her?"

Joanne looked to both of them.

"No one has told me anything," Joanne tossed her pen on the desk and crossed her arms. "Not a word for three months, or is it four now?"

Rick half smiled.

"May I?" He grabbed a chair.

"No reason to be formal." She couldn't figure out this new version of Rick Jones. But she wasn't the same version of Joanne he'd last seen, either.

He sat. Cleared his throat, "First, I apologize for not getting hold of you. I knew my guys would..."

She glanced at Roberts, still leaning in her doorway.

Roberts cocked his head, like *give Rick a chance.*

"They'd do their best," Rick continued.

"You knew he was alive?" she addressed Roberts with cool tact. "You could've said something. Anything..."

Rick had never seen her this confident, nor had he felt this vulnerable before.

She wasn't buying it. "If you could get in touch... and didn't— not acceptable. I pay your firm for their services. I hired you to..."

"Let me go back to that day." He rubbed his forehead, "I took my eyes off you when I shouldn't have. When the power was flickering. You remember, the situation deteriorated into chaos rapidly."

Joanne agreed. "I don't blame you for getting out. For running. It was awful."

He appeared stricken, then teared up. "You think I ran?"

Roberts wasn't leaving the doorway.

"Tell her," he urged Rick.

Joanne and Rick both turned to Roberts as if to say, SHUT UP.

"What should I think? It's not like you've been communicating," she was pissed. She trained her eyes on Roberts again, "If you already know what's going on, get out. And shut the door. I'm waiting for him to say it."

She turned back to Rick.

Rick nodded to Roberts, who left reluctantly, shutting the door behind him.

Joanne sighed. "You were with Liebold last I saw you... then chaos, as you noted."

"I had my concerns about the security of our location, during the power surges," Rick sat back. "Liebold followed. He shut the entry door behind him, to reassure me it was functioning. Then the power surged again and the door was sealed shut."

She was beginning to get the picture. Rick was too pained to speak for a moment.

"I couldn't see where you were," she told him, filling in the silence. "I saw Humberto kill a guard and make his way out of the secured area that led through God knows where? When I got to the parking lot, the Hummer was gone..."

He was visibly horrified by her account as she trailed off. Better not to go into further detail about how she got outside, she decided.

"The gate was gone," he said finally, reliving the moment. "It was gone. I couldn't get that goddamned door open, I couldn't see you, or cover you. I could hear alarms, gunfire... and I just had to hope the guards had it under control. So I took the alternate route, I got outside to the Hummer and was going to crash it into the yard. But the gate was already gone, and those animals were everywhere. They tried to take the Hummer..."

Joanne swallowed the lump forming in her throat.

A moment passed before Rick went on, "I ran over a few inmates and they backed off. Then I got hold of one piece of shit who was trying to outrun me..."

Rick's memory engulfed him and he was back in the moment. Rick had his gun so far down the asshole's throat he couldn't make out what he was saying.

"Vasquez!" Rick repeated, removing the barrel of the gun from the slightly smaller man's mouth and shoving it into his left eyelid.

"He's gone, he left with the girl..."

Rick had dropped the guy where they stood and was back in the Hummer, racing onto the highway in the rain.

He blinked himself back to the present. "I thought Vasquez had you. I looked for you everywhere—in ditches. SWAT passed me heading in to COR. The media was already setting up on the perimeter. I knew you couldn't be far, so I kept retracing... and retracing..." His eyes spilled tears, his voice breaking. "I turned on the radio to get a clue what was happening."

Joanne had never seen him like this. He had to wait several moments before he could go on.

"There was a live feed... and I heard your voice. I was so grateful you were safe." He took out a handkerchief and blew his nose. "I couldn't live with myself knowing I took you there, and I failed to protect you."

She grabbed a tissue and wiped her own watering eyes.

She thought about George begging her to stay. Zach apologizing for his part in setting Collins up. This felt too familiar.

"You *accompanied* me there. It was my choice to go, or you never would've taken me there." She blinked tears from her eyes, "We both know that."

"I didn't do my job." Rick looked away, "I wanted to make it up to you, Joanne. I went to Colombia."

"You... what?" Joanne was stunned.

There was a long silence. She wanted to scream, or hit him. Or crawl into his lap and kiss him. Maybe all of the above. Her heart pounded.

Colombia?

"They're all home," he said finally.

Clark Roberts opened the door, as if on cue.

"Joanne, please come to the lobby."

Joanne didn't understand. She tried to go to Rick, but he waved her off.

"You need to go with Clark, and I need a minute..."

Clark gestured for her to follow him, "Rick's not going anywhere. We need you in the lobby."

Reluctantly, she followed Roberts.

She was greeted by dozens of women, children and their families—holding banners thanking her.

They cheered and ran to her.

"Thank you for saving my life." One woman fell to her knees and hugged Joanne's leg.

Joanne was confused and overwhelmed.

"Rick did this?" She turned to Roberts.

"He did it for you."

Joanne was astonished. She felt weak in the knees.

"He rescued or negotiated the release of every single woman the Vasquez cartel captured."

She looked for Rick. She wanted to share this moment with him.

It was truly *his* moment.

"Greet your people, Joanne. Rick can tell you everything later," Roberts said, as if he'd read her thoughts.

She recognized many of their faces. She had studied their profiles, memorized their pictures.

"Debra," she hugged her.

"Simone. Susan." They cried as she spoke their names.

It was a homecoming.

She heard a giggle. She turned.

"Who was that?" She asked several people, "I heard a little girl's voice."

One of the appreciative parents said, "It is your little girl I bet. She's an angel now."

Joanne smiled and nodded.

She hugged everyone. One by one.

Jackie and Josh beamed at their new baby girl while Joanne and Rick marveled at the sweet bundle in pink.

"May I?" Rick asked.

Josh grinned, "I insist."

He handed the little girl to Rick, who cooed and made faces at the baby.

"I think she looks like you both."

Joanne was taken by how animated and even foolish Rick looked. He continued to evolve in ways she'd never anticipated.

"What is her name?" Joanne asked.

Jackie was evasive. "Josh, Joanne wants to know the baby's name."

Josh begged off, "You tell her."

"I hope you don't mind," Jackie began...

"Okay," Josh interrupted. "It sounds funny when you put it together, but we've really thought this over."

Jackie laughed. "Well, her middle name for sure. But Joanne, the only reason Josh and I found each other is because of what happened to you and my dad."

"Well, at least something wonderful resulted," Joanne acknowledged, swallowing hard. "You might want to skip that story until she's older."

Jackie nodded, holding onto Joanne's hand. "You can tell her."

Rick made more raspberries at the baby. "Enough build up. Let's hear it."

Jackie still hesitated. "We came up with Zabel to honor my mother and father, but chose Marquel as her first name. Zabel is her middle name. Marquel Zabel," though out loud it sounded like she was saying "Marquel's a belle".

Josh started singing, "Marquel Za-bel. These are words that go together well. My Marquel."

"The Beatles song." Rick began singing with Josh as he returned the infant to her father, "I love you. I love you. I love you." Then he looked at Joanne and continued, "That's all I want to say."

The nurse came in. "That's quite a serenade."

Joanne was touched, but couldn't let them name their daughter Marquel. Not after all that had happened.

"Jackie, I love you. Thank you. I love your daughter, but I have to ask you to reconsider. For her sake." Joanne moved to where the men were and kissed the baby on her forehead, "I've done enough damage to the name."

"My father loved you dearly. We love you—We'll call her Markie for short. Your daughter will be her guardian angel," Jackie insisted.

"This is a lovely honor... but your child needs to leave her own mark."

Jackie smiled. "Mark. See, you aren't even trying, and her name is there. Look at the good your foundation is doing. That you and Rick are doing."

Josh brought the baby to Joanne.

"Hey grandma. Hold me." He placed baby Marquel in Joanne's arms, "Besides, given your notoriety you can't expect this is the only child in the world bearing the name."

She didn't hear the last words Josh had said as she held the baby close. This felt so familiar. Joanne hadn't considered they'd accept her as a grandmother.

"Marquel," Joanne said just above a whisper. She rocked her.

Rick knelt beside them. He couldn't believe how beautiful Joanne looked at that moment.

"What do you think grandma?"

She nuzzled little Marquel close.

CHAPTER TWENTY-SEVEN

Judith looked at her watch. Greta was late. They had a reservation at Greta's favorite restaurant, the Silver Seahorse. Everyone there knew Greta. She took clients there. She was a regular even before she met Judith.

The restaurant wasn't far from their Sullivan Canyon home near Brentwood. It was their ninth anniversary of living together in the home.

The house was a wedding gift they gave each other, though they could not legally marry. They had spoken vows and had the home blessed when they moved in. Their Nouveau modern ranch home had scenic views and occasional wildlife that happened onto the property. Their décor was clean minimalism, resembling a favorite Georgia O' Keeffe home they both admired.

Tonight, Judith wanted to surprise Greta with a gift they had talked about for a long time.

Judith called Ken's office.

"When did Greta leave?"

Ken couldn't remember. "Gosh, hours ago. We had a casting call—it was awful. Like a marionette show. Wooden, stiff auditions. We didn't like anyone! God, I needed a toddy after that. She wanted to go shopping but I couldn't think about it. Off she went."

Judith didn't want to ask, but under the circumstances. "Did Greta join you for that toddy?"

"Yes. But not to worry. She took a cab." Ken yawned, "Come to think of it, I'd better call one."

"Ken it's 9 pm," Judith wondered if Evan was equally worried.

Ken laughed. "Evan is in bed reading by now."

"Be safe, Ken." Judith next called the restaurant. "This is Judith Wright. Greta and I had a reservation for this evening..."

"Greta's waiting for you. She's a wee bit drunk," The hostess laughed.

"I'm on my way." Judith took a deep breath, thankful Greta was there. "Could you serve her water or start her on appetizers."

"We'll do our best," the young woman replied and hung up.

Rick brought Joanne breakfast in bed.

They'd found themselves making out after they returned from the hospital. One thing led to another, but she stopped him.

"I'm not sure about this." She set the tray aside.

"About what?" Rick was puzzled.

"I think we've crossed the line."

Joanne got up and took the tray to the kitchen.

He followed her.

"We had something last night." He tried to take her hand, but she withdrew.

"I feel awkward, Rick. We were just acting on the sexual tension we have living here." She tightened her robe.

He smiled. "Felt great."

"Doesn't make it right," Joanne said. "I went through this with Zach. He was my doctor. He broke his ethics. It was a disaster, as you know."

His eyes searched hers. "Joanne, I want to marry you."

"Did you hear what I just said?" she asked.

"Did you hear what I just said?" he echoed.

"I'm firing you, Rick. I'm firing you and your firm. I can't do this again."

Joanne left the room.

Rick stood there, stunned.

Finally, he went back to his room.

He didn't know where to begin. He unplugged his scanner.

He sat on the bed and rubbed his eyes. "Zach, brother, I'm beginning to understand."

Jackie and Josh dropped off baby Marquel with Joanne.

"We're going to Dr. Clay's housewarming. I'm sure we won't be there long."

Jackie kissed the baby on the head. She tied the turquoise cross and chain she wore at her wedding to back of the baby's car seat.

Josh handed Joanne a prescription.

Before she could ask, he said, "Oh, sorry. Jackie wanted me to write down the address and phone numbers for you, in case you need to reach us. That's all I had."

Josh kissed his daughter.

"Have a good time," Joanne encouraged the couple.

"Call if you need anything," Jackie said. "We'll come right back."

Josh laughed. "Or not."

Jackie elbowed her husband.

"Okay," Josh rubbed his ribs. "Be good for Grandma, Markie."

Jackie kissed Marquel again and hugged Joanne. "Thank you. I miss her already and I'm not out the door." Jackie's eyes teared up.

Joanne was touched by the young mother's heart. She could see herself and George in the two of them.

"We're going to watch some Muppet videos and read stories. Even if she sleeps through it all." Joanne had prepared for this night.

Josh tugged at Jackie's sleeve. "Babe, time to go."

Jackie agreed.

The sleeping baby stretched her little arms upward. Then relaxed. A smile crept across her face.

"That's gas," Josh said. "She takes after me."

"Go." Jackie pushed Josh.

"We'll call you when we get to Clay's house," Josh said. "You must pick up on the first ring. Don't go to the bathroom or anything..."

Jackie rolled her eyes. "Okay, we're leaving."

Jackie kissed her daughter one more time. "I love you."

Joanne rocked Marquel and held her tenderly. The baby's pink hand gripped her pinky finger.

Joanne's apartment had an almost golden luminosity. The lights seemed to cast a soft yellow radiance and Joanne felt a presence she hadn't experienced before.

She wondered if the neighbors might see a Kinkade-like glow through her windows. Joanne had seen Thomas Kinkade's work, but never thought where the inspiration might come from.

She was now living alone. She missed Rick, but felt at peace.

After a bottle and a diaper change, they read a book.

Time passed quickly.

She was glad Josh didn't worry about calling. She didn't want the phone to disrupt their embrace. Marquel would go home soon and Joanne didn't want this special time to end.

The phone rang.

Joanne laughed. "Marquel, Mommy and Daddy just can't live without you..." She picked up the phone. "We're doing fine."

She smiled at Marquel who stretched a bit.

"Joanne Manning?" The caller sounded official.

"This is she," Joanne was surprised. She whispered, "It's not your parents."

"There is an LAPD officer at your door. I just wanted to be sure you were home. Is anyone with you?"

Joanne was startled, "My... granddaughter." She hadn't said it until then.

"Are you on a cordless phone?" The caller asked.

"Yes, and I'm holding the baby." Joanne's voice cracked. "What's wrong?"

"Can you place the baby in a carrier or crib and come to the door?"

Joanne began to shake. She could feel a lump rising in her throat. Her whole body began to quiver. She placed the phone on the table and knelt, placing the baby in the carrier.

She looked for the glow. Was it there? She took a few deep breaths.

"Are you still there?" the caller wanted her to stay on the line.

She heard 'there' and realized it was the phone.

She grabbed it. "I'm here. Please tell me what is going on?"

Was it Rick? Did something happen?

This couldn't be.

CHAPTER TWENTY-EIGHT

Joanne opened the door. Isabel was standing there with two LAPD officers and a social worker.

"I'm here for my granddaughter," Isabel muttered. Her makeup was streaked, her speech slurred.

Joanne breathed a sigh of relief. Rick must be okay.

She couldn't figure out what Isabel was up to. It seemed jealousy had reared its ugly head again.

"Jackie and Josh will be..."

Joanne couldn't finish before Isabel screamed, "God damn you!"

Isabel lunged for Joanne but was caught by the male officer.

Joanne was shocked. She couldn't understand how Isabel commandeered the police into taking the baby before her parents got back.

The female officer spoke, "There's been an accident."

Isabel wrestled with the officer and screamed at Joanne. "They're dead! It's your fault. You curse everything!" She shook uncontrollably.

Joanne fell to her knees. The social worker caught her.

The officer continued calmly, "Jacqueline and Joshua Burke were fatally injured when their car was struck by a drunk driver. They and the driver of the other vehicle were killed."

Just then the baby woke and started crying hysterically.

Isabel shrieked, "And that baby's name is going to be changed! DO YOU HEAR ME!"

The baby cried louder.

The social worker moved toward the carrier and picked up little Marquel.

"Isabel Herlbert is the next of kin."

Joanne shook her head violently. "Jackie would want... want... would want..." She couldn't trust herself to say it.

Isabel struggled with the officer. "Let go of me."

He held on to her, "You need to remain calm."

The front door was still open.

"I heard on the scanner."

Joanne knew that voice. Her mind couldn't connect it.

The officers turned and gave a nod. There was a familiarity among them.

Joanne felt lightheaded. She wasn't certain what to do next.

Rick entered.

Joanne ran to Rick.

He held her. "I got here as soon as I could. Oh my God, Joanne. I'm so sorry."

Isabel sobbed uncontrollably. "...NO!" She began hyperventilating and collapsed.

The female officer called for an ambulance.

The baby screamed louder.

"May I," Joanne pulled away from Rick and the social worker handed Joanne the baby.

Almost immediately the infant began to settle down.

Rick stroked the baby's head.

"We have to help Isabel," Joanne pleaded.

Rick moved toward the officers and discussed the situation.

A siren was heard outside.

Joanne rocked little Marquel. "Mommy and Daddy love you. I love you."

The paramedics came in and began assessing Isabel.

CHAPTER TWENTY-NINE

"I can't believe we're doing this." Greta was thrilled by Judith's anniversary gift.

Judith looked at her checklist. "I think we're going to need to grab a few things."

Greta and Judith packed for their trip around the world.

Greta was grateful Judith didn't lecture her about drinking. She was afraid she'd ruined their anniversary dinner. She loved Judith dearly and wanted to make her proud, but relapsed.

"I have one other surprise for you," Judith said.

Greta couldn't imagine. "Tell me."

"I've sold my practice. I'm retiring."

Greta was speechless.

"Oh, and Ken and Evan are meeting us in Paris, after our stay at the treehouse in Kenya."

Greta grabbed Judith and kissed her. "I love you. But you've never wanted to retire. What about Joanne and all the other patients?"

Judith sat on the edge of the bed and put her pen and paper on the bedside table.

"Greta darling, I'm not getting any younger." She smiled, "I've been there for everyone else. Now I want to be there for you."

Greta sat next to Judith and put her head on her shoulder. "You're making me cry."

Joanne and Rick paced the emergency room waiting area.

Joanne began to cry. "I keep expecting Josh to come out and tell us what's going on."

Rick held her.

"Where is Lyle?" Joanne rubbed her nose on her sleeve.

Rick was beside himself. He hadn't been able to convince the social worker to release the baby to he and Joanne. Baby Marquel was taken to foster care.

He could barely speak. In all of his years as a soldier he never felt as helpless as he did at this moment.

"There's no one left." Joanne sat in the corner of the room and rocked herself, "We have to get Marquel. Ohmygod."

Rick joined her. He couldn't be the strong one this time.

He was spent. He held his head and broke down.

Joanne looked at Rick.

He'd been her rock—rescued her, protected her, danced with her, laughed with her, asked her to marry him.

She needed to find the resolve to help him.

"I love you, Rick." Joanne knelt down next to him.

He drew away.

Joanne repeated herself. "I love you. I was wrong to reject you."

Rick shook his head. "No, Joanne. You're reacting out of fear now. You should be very proud of yourself. You know yourself. I'm not getting in the way of your progress."

Joanne's eyes washed with tears. "But Rick, I do know myself. Finally!"

He wanted to kiss her and hold her tight. But he knew he'd have to say goodbye.

She moved to hug him. He wouldn't let her.

Joanne sat at his feet. "I'm not letting you go, Rick Jones."

He dropped his head and cried.

They both stayed silent until the doctor came in.

"Are you Isabel Herlbert's next of kin?" He asked them.

Joanne stood, "She's my sister."

Rick was surprised by her lie.

"Isabel has had a severe stroke. She may need surgery to remove a blockage from her right carotid artery." The doctor paused and looked at some notes, "We'll need a signature..."

"You can't make that decision," Rick interrupted.

Joanne's mouth fell open. "Do you actually think Jackie would agree with you?"

The doctor excused himself for a moment while they talked.

Rick spoke softly, "Joanne, you are not this woman's sister. If they find out and somehow Isabel recovers, she'll sue your ass and take the baby."

Joanne was adamant, "Provided I get custody! Who is going to speak up for Isabel? Lyle isn't her husband anymore. He bought her out. I'm doing what Jackie would if she were here."

"We have to wait for Lyle. He knows her better..." Rick insisted.

Joanne threw up her hands. "How long do we wait?"

The doctor returned. "She's stabilized for tonight. However, it would be in Isabel's best interest if we could do the procedure in the morning."

Joanne looked at Rick.

Rick walked out.

"We're waiting for another family member before we sign anything," Joanne took the doctor's card. "I'll call you in a few hours."

The doctor reminded her that Isabel needed the procedure to avoid another stroke—time being of the essence. The doctor left.

Joanne stood silent in the waiting room. She wondered where Rick had gone, but couldn't focus her thoughts long enough to prioritize anything.

A svelte-looking man approached her.

"I'm trying to find..." he trailed off.

They stared at each other for a moment.

"Joanne?" Lyle asked.

They had not officially met.

Joanne was relieved. "Lyle?"

He nodded.

"We need your help."

"Joanne, I'm so very sorry for yours and Isabel's loss." He was frank.

"What does that mean?" Joanne could barely keep her face from twitching as she tried to control her emotions.

"It means I'm truly sorry," he said. "I'm here because you called. Tell me about Isabel."

"She's in need of surgery. She had a stroke."

He nodded.

Joanne was at a loss for what to do next. Should she try to see Isabel... For Jackie's sake?

Lyle ever the professional. "She'll need a guardian appointed. Do you want that responsibility, Joanne?"

At that moment the fluorescent light behind her flickered and buzzed.

She turned. It was George, she knew. She could feel it.

"No. She doesn't," Rick was back. He offered his hand to Lyle. The men held their positions.

Relieved, Joanne stood between them. "Then who?"

"Herman Hause has stepped up," Rick said.

Joanne was confused.

Lyle sat and crossed his legs. "They are good friends. I can see that. He would be a good conservator of her assets," he agreed.

Rick ignored Lyle.

"Did you mean what you said?" Rick looked into Joanne's eyes.

She nodded.

At that moment the fluorescent light behind Rick went out. Joanne choked up. She knew George was at peace.

Lyle looked at his watch. "I'll not be attending a service for Jackie and Josh, but I'll be happy to contribute to a trust fund for the baby. They were a sweet couple."

Then Lyle stood. He shook Rick's hand and touched Joanne's shoulder. "Isabel has enough of my money to live comfortably, goodnight."

Rick turned to face Joanne.

"I accept your proposal," he searched her eyes. Hopeful.

"I love you so much." Joanne wrapped her arms and legs around Rick.

They lingered in a long passionate kiss.

Rick broke from the kiss. "Don't ask me how he did it, but the baby is at Lou's house," Rick grinned.

Joanne gasped. "Why didn't you tell me?"

She kissed him again and again, all over his face.

"I called Lou when I was on my way to your place, and again after I walked out. I just got off the phone with him when I saw you talking to Lyle.

Rick gave her another a long, hard kiss. He put her down.

"Tell me," Joanne caught her breath.

"Lou checked in at LAPD when he didn't hear back from me." Rick smiled, "He called in a favor."

Joanne's eyes got big.

"He said it was the right kind of favor. No drug lords involved," Rick kissed her forehead.

She took a deep breath. "What do we do next?"

"We go to the courthouse in the morning and make this legal. Then we adopt little Marquel." Rick looked her in the eye. "Lou agreed to inform Ken, Evan, Judith and Greta about... everything."

She teared up. "Can we move to another state?"

He kissed her nose. "Do you still have those travel magazines?"

She nodded.

"You were looking for a place where Marquel would like to live."

Joanne was astonished. "I did say that."

Rick closed his eyes. He said a silent prayer that Joanne would be okay, that they would be okay, and the baby would be okay.

"What about Isabel?" Joanne realized this wasn't going to be as simple as Rick hoped.

"Hermann Hause will work with us. Trust me. Those guys loved Jackie. And they adore Isabel."

Joanne knew he was right.

Rick was a realist. "We have to plan a funeral, Joanne. Are you able to do this?"

Joanne teared up again. "I want to do this right for little Marquel, if it is possible..."

"Of course," Rick said.

She threw her head back and tried to figure how to best say it. "This sounds morbid, but if they aren't disfigured. I'd like to use the funeral photographer that Jackie used for Zach's service."

Rick didn't follow. He wasn't certain what she was talking about.

Joanne swallowed hard. "When I was still hospitalized in a coma, and Zach passed... Jackie had photos taken of Zach in his casket."

"Marquel's a baby. Photos from the wedding will serve as her memories," Rick was confident.

"Are you sure, Rick?" Joanne wasn't. "Those photos gave me peace."

Rick didn't agree. "I'm going to be your husband, right?"

She nodded.

"I'm going to be Marquel's dad, too."

She nodded again, smiling through her tears.

"Then we'll respect Jackie and Josh differently than Jackie did for you," he studied Joanne's expression.

"I trust you," Joanne smiled.

"God, I love you, Joanne." Rick kissed her again. "And I love Marquel and Jackie and Josh... and even Isabel."

Joanne laughed. "Poor Isabel. I'd buy a nursing home and take great care of her... for Jackie."

Rick shook his head. "You would... but Hause will do a better job caring for her. You need to focus on our little girl."

"We need to focus..." she corrected him.

"I stand corrected," Rick acknowledged.

"Oh, we have to call the doctor back," Joanne fished the doctor's card out of her pocket.

"Hause will." Rick took the card.

"I feel better already. I was afraid I'd have to carry on as Isabel's sister." Joanne wiped the tears from her eyes. "How many hours til the courthouse opens?"

"Enough that we could grab breakfast, a shower and a celebratory romp in the sack." He winked.

That wink...

"I'm glad you don't work for me anymore. I wouldn't want to sexually harass you."

Rick threw his head back and laughed. "I told you I wouldn't press charges."

Joanne kissed his nose.

"Maybe the shower after the romp?" She suggested.

"Deal."

ACKNOWLEDGEMENTS

First, I'd like to thank my sister Ellen Williams for being a great editor. I am blessed by your talent and love.

Thank you to Lisa Despain, my book formatter and marketer. She's pushed me out of my comfort zone this year and called my bluff on ideas I whined about needing. As a result, I have grown my social media and reader fan base at a surprising rate. Lisa's businesses are Ebookconverting.com and book2 bestseller.com—I highly recommend her to any author.

To Tom Hillman who manages my emilyskinnerbooks.com and ewskinner.com sites. You make me look good. Thank you!

To Judy Roe, who read the first book Marquel many years ago. She changed my life with these words: "When are you going to write another novel? You are one of my favorite authors."

Judy's sincere encouragement motivated me to keep going. Others came later, Robyn Fairbanks, Roxanne Smith, Roberta Terranova, Kim Salter, Millie Zager may she rest in peace, Marylou Bourdow, Marcia Engle, Joyce Huslander, Caitlin Poley, Jodi Poley, Theresa Moser, Kathy Durnell, Carrie Vaniero and more.

To Lani Skuthorpe whom I met through Bunny Cates on Twitter, Lani lives in Australia. She is a Team George fan from the first book and beta read the second book of the series for me. She has moved from being a reader to writing under the name Elle Thorpe. You must look her up!

To all of my readers, it is a pleasure to share my characters and their adventures with you. This third book was a joy to write. I'd love to hear your favorite characters and moments in any of the books. Please contact me at emilyauthor7@icloud.com.

For the book reviewers and bloggers, God bless you! Sharing is caring. The time you take to help authors is immeasurable.

A big shout out to two women who help me promote: Suleika Santana of All About Books Divas on Facebook or https://www.facebook.com/bookninjas2 and Michelle Bowman of WLK Book Promotions http://www.wlkbookpromotions.com.

Please forgive me if I missed anyone!!!!!!

To our daughters Marquel Skinner and Blair Skinner, for the Marquel book trailer you made, it is amazing!

To actor Eric Roberts who starred in the book trailer, we are honored by your performance, talent and generous consideration.

To my mother Barbara Williams for her Hollywood obsession as we were growing up. I love you. I have nothing but fond memories of watching you buy your weekly fix of movie magazines, as well as scraping together enough change and returning soda bottles so we could all go to movies.

To my best friend and husband Tom Skinner, I love you. Thank you for listening and providing great feedback on my story ideas.

OTHER WORKS BY EMILY W. SKINNER

Novels by Emily W. Skinner

Marquel

Marquel's Dilemma

Marquel's Redemption

Booktrailer:
Marquel book trailer on YouTube—
featuring actor Eric Roberts & Marquel Skinner
www.youtube.com/watch?v=6e6O7iYqeVQ

Young Adult Novels by E. W. Skinner

St. Blair: Children of the Night

St. Blair: Sybille's Reign

St Blair: The Diary of St. Blair

Sign up for email updates at:

www.emilyskinnerbooks.com

Follow Emily on:

www.facebook.com/emilyskinnerbooks

www.twitter.com/emilyauthor

http://www.thefilmmom.blogspot.com/

https://www.goodreads.com/author/show/
6982753.Emily_W_Skinner

ABOUT THE AUTHOR

Emily Skinner lives in Tampa Bay, Florida with her husband, Tom. In addition to writing, she also enjoys selling advertising, and working with their daughters, Marquel Skinner and Blair Skinner on their film and acting projects.

www.ingramcontent.com/pod-product-compliance
Lightning Source LLC
Chambersburg PA
CBHW031952130726
47905CB00003BA/768